If You Please, President Lincoln
President
Lincoln

Books by Harriette Gillem Robinet

Ride the Red Cycle

Children of the Fire

Mississippi Chariot

If You Please, President Lincoln

If You Please, President Lincoln

Harriette Gillem Robinet

A *Jean Karl Book*
Atheneum Books for Young Readers

Atheneum Books for Young Readers
An imprint of Simon & Schuster Children's Publishing Division
1230 Avenue of the Americas
New York, New York 10020

Book design by Laura Hammond Hough
The text of this book is set in Goudy

FIRST EDITION
Printed in the United States of America
10 9 8 7 6 5 4 3 2 1

Robinet, Harriette.
        If you please, president Lincoln / Harriette Gillem Robinet.—
1st ed.
                p.   cm.
        "A Jean Karl book."
        Summary: Shortly after the Christmas of 1863, fourteen-year-old Moses
thinks he is beginning a new free life when he becomes part of a group of other former
slaves headed for a small island off the coast of Haiti.
        ISBN 0-915793-86-5
        [1. Afro-Americans—Fiction.   2. Slavery—Fiction.} I. Title.
pz7.R553If 1995
[Fic]—dc20   95-2126
                                                                                                              CIP
                                                                                                              AC

To my brother, Henry Alvin Gray Gillem, Sr., and his wife, Naomi Mauney Gillem, and their children: Cecelia Gillem Torres, Angela Rose Gillem, and Henry Alvin Gray Gillem, Jr., and to their grandchildren.

I acknowledge my dear friends, Rheba Galloway Fearn and James Earnest Fearn, for reading the manuscript and correcting boating terms.

I acknowledge our son, Stephen Robinet, who found and photocopied early and recent material on Haiti.

I acknowledge my husband, McLouis Robinet, for always being my first reader, and for his constant loving support without which I could not write.

And I acknowledge the librarians of the Oak Park Public Library and of Chicago's Newberry Library and Harold Washington Library's Special Collection for their courteous resourcefulness.

Oh, how I hope his excellency President Abraham Lincoln and his most honorable Congress read my account. For I write the story of more than four hundred hapless souls of African descent who were victims of a scheme: a cruel plan of taking us from these United States to Isle à Vache, otherwise known as Cow Island of the Republic of Hayti.

And, as sure as the warm sun gives light, my story is true, while accounts by others will be bent and twisted like green willow saplings in the shade.

For me, Cow Island hardships can be expressed as follows: Out of treachery, truth; out of strangers, family; out of struggle, strength; and out of sufferings, understanding sweeter than milk and honey in heaven.

But first, I must needs tell you who I am.

From birth I have had the curse of slavery stamped on me. Notwithstanding, I am able to read and write because I was taught by no less than a priest of the Society of Jesus, although such teaching was, in truth, illegal at that time.

Let me begin at a beginning so that you may know the story of a slave boy, and of how I arrived in Annapolis,

Maryland, and boarded that clipper ship to Cow Island. At the time my account begins, my age was fourteen years, as nearly as Aunt Rebekah could tell. And my name was Moses of Father Fitzpatrick.

Christmas Eve of 1863 found me and Aunt Rebekah kneeling in the chilly sacristy of St. Mary's of the Sea Church. Our church and home in one was in Maryland on the eastern shore of the Potomac River. In silence my Christmas prayers raised to heaven like lavender incense from the swinging censer. I reasoned that if our gracious God could read my sinful heart—as Father Fitzpatrick always told me—then God could certainly hear my silent prayers.

However, Aunt Rebekah muttered her prayers aloud. Perchance she thought God was growing deaf as she was, and needed to hear better. She was a woman perhaps in her sixties. I understood that she and Father Fitzpatrick were only one year apart in age. Short, she was great in heart and great in size. I had looked down on her from my twelfth year. Now that I was fourteen, her head only reached my shoulder.

Her turbans were always sunset red, her aprons were white like milk from the cow, and dark skirts always modestly covered her sturdy ankles.

Her girth was greater than the oak tree planted more than a century ago in St. Mary's churchyard. So great was her size that when the doctor told Father Fitzpatrick that she had three large abdominal tumors, no one could have suspected. Those tumors caused her great pain. Furthermore, the doctor said her healing must needs come from heaven, as he could bring about no cure.

And so, that Christmas Eve, I prayed for tumor healing.

Aloud, Aunt Rebekah prayed a political speech. Father Fitzpatrick would have found her prayers bold, impudent, and sinful. And she prayed aloud so that I could hear and be influenced. I wished I could put fingers in my ears!

"Lord," she muttered, "our honorable Congress last year freed those slaves living in Washington, D.C. And still in Maryland we be slaves. And, Lord, the Emancipation Proclamation freed those slaves living in rebellious states. And still in Maryland we be slaves." She winced in pain and sighed before continuing.

"Not so much for me, Lord—for I be weak and old and headed for your heavenly home—but for the boy, Moses of Father Fitzpatrick, Lord, let freedom ring!"

I suppose she called my name in case God was absentminded and thought she might mean some other boy. Her prayer was sinful because none of Father Fitzpatrick's slaves was allowed to talk about freedom.

Sunday after Sunday Father preached to us at Mass. He said, "Christ healed the ear of Malchus's slave, but he didn't free him. St. Paul sent a runaway slave back to his master. And, the good Father would say, shaking a finger in our faces, "that same St. Paul told slaves in Corinth not to be concerned about being free!"

I obeyed the good Father. All I desired was to follow orders well, but Aunt Rebekah wanted me to think for myself. I was not concerned to be free, but Aunt Rebekah was concerned for me. "Moses," she would whisper, "we all God's children, and we all deserve to be free!"

I am telling you this so you will understand my feelings, who I was, and who I have come to be. That night I felt guilty and sinful just listening to Aunt Rebekah. However, she was the only mother I had ever known. Nothing could make me act disrespectful, and nothing could make me leave her.

After her prayer, she heaved a great sigh. The sacristy where we knelt on the cold hard floor was a narrow room behind the altar of the church. The walls were covered with oaken cabinets for vestments, and in the corner a dry sink for washing the sacred vessels rested in the hands of a marble angel. A door from either side of the sacristy led onto the altar of St. Mary's; a third door led outside.

The door on our side of the sacristy was open just a slit for us to see the altar; this Father Fitzpatrick allowed only on Christmas, Easter, and Pentecost. In the morning he would say a separate Mass outdoors in the rice lands for field slaves. Field slaves could not hear Mass in the church as we two house slaves did that night.

Inside the church now I spied white men, women, and children standing in all their Christmas finery. They wore blues and greens and black; they wore velvets and laces and fine woolen broadcloth. Some highly successful men carried sable top hats. Women wore bonnets with Christmas bows beneath their chins. Children squirmed and yawned. I suspected they wore too tight shoes, scratchy starch in shirts, and itchy lace on dresses.

At the end of Christmas Eve Mass, bells ran out as the recessional began. People sang, "Silent night, holy night, all is calm, all is bright."

I scrambled to my feet and helped Aunt Rebekah

stand. I reached for our black cloaks. With one last glance at the candlelit, incense-fragrant glory for white people inside St. Mary's of the Sea, we hastened outside.

Sparkling crystals of snow danced in the midnight sky. "Praise the Lord!" whispered Aunt Rebekah. "Snow! Gift of Christmas angels." For her everything was a gift of angels.

She twitched my arm to stand still like some church statue. I threw back my head and let drifting white snowflakes wet my brown face. Only when they sifted cold as freezing fingers into the stiff white collar that I wore did I in turn twitch her arm to trudge on.

My stiff white collar was above a starched white jabot with lace edging. I wore a well-fitted black jacket cut away to the front, and black, tight-fitting pants. Likewise Aunt Rebekah wore a fine dark blue dress with full white collar and, of course, her red turban. We were dressed to serve Father Fitzpatrick and his guests late Christmas Eve supper. They were soon ready.

As I entered the dining room, a tap on the shoulder from Aunt Rebekah reminded me not to stare at Father's guests. I held my gaze upon the wide-board refectory floor. Notwithstanding, I noted his aged father by his gold cane, his younger sister in last Christmas's cranberry red dress, two other priests, and of course Father Fitzpatrick.

I amused myself by thinking that, were we not in the midst of the War Between the States, Miss Emily Fitzpatrick—the good Father's sister—would not be dressed thus. To wear any fancy dress twice was not to her liking. To wear the same cranberry red dress on two Christmas Eves must have pained like a dagger in her pride.

I served roast lamb, potatoes, rice, dinner rolls, stewed tomatoes, and for dessert, plum pudding. The aroma of such good eatings made my eyes water. Hunger gnawed at my innards.

As I poured coffee, from the corner of my eye I saw Aunt Rebekah bend over in pain. The last cup being served, I pushed the swinging door into the kitchen. She beckoned.

"Water," she whispered. "You'll know." And she pointed to the bucket for the well. With effort, she straighted up.

I hesitated but for a moment, there being two buckets, one within the other. She gestured for me to move quickly. Without my cloak I trotted out, buckets heavy in hand.

Cold air stung my face and hands. Cold quickly penetrated my garments, and yet I felt satisfied. Aunt Rebekah had allowed me this sinful disobedience, which I suspected that she did on many occasions. Satisfied to be doing wrong? My only discomfort was in the thought that she herself was too ill to carry it out.

The inner, good-smelling bucket I placed among the bushes at the edge of the yard, the outer bucket I carried to the well.

"Merry Christmas," called a soft voice from the bushes. I was much too near the rectory to answer safely.

The voice was Porter's. Aunt Rebekah had sent food—lamb and other victuals—in the bucket. Porter was a field hand, a slave working on Father Fitzpatrick's rice lands. During the winter there was precious little work to do. About twenty grown-up slaves belonged there, and perchance as many children, but the war had changed things. Of those forty slaves, about seven were still there for next spring's rice planting, and among the seven, three were children younger than I.

Yet every Sunday about twenty slaves attended Mass. The good Father knew few by name, and he had laid off his overseer during this wartime winter, so any neighboring slaves could fill in. The field slaves must have had a plan to fool him.

The War Between the States had certainly put loyal slaves like me to the test. I didn't approve of how other slaves wandered about as if they were already free. Since there was so little work in the winter, some visited mothers, fathers, sisters, brothers, husbands, wives on other plantations in broad daylight! Others ran away for good.

Father Fitzpatrick preached their duty to serve God as slaves, yet one by one they ran away. Aunt Rebekah wished the same for me, sending me time and again to Washington for spices and seafood and sewing notions. She wanted me to make a life for myself as a free person, instead of just obeying orders as a slave.

She would whisper, "You a smart boy what can read and write. Go on to Washington for me, but don't come back!"

I loved the trips up from the Chesapeake Bay along the Potomac River to the great city wharves of Washington, D.C. But once my purchasing business was done in the city, I returned on some neighbor's seacraft.

Much to Aunt Rebekah's disappointment.

Now with water in my bucket, I opened the kitchen door to return. Inside, Aunt Rebekah cowered under the pointed finger of Father Fitzpatrick.

The good Father said in a low voice, "What did you send by the boy?"

He was whispering, but his anger was thundering loud. You see, he did not wish to spoil his field slaves with food such as we ate. From the storeroom keeper, they each received a half cup of cornmeal, a fatty curl of bacon, and sometimes one egg for their daily fare. The good Father's theory was that the harder a slave worked, the less that slave should eat.

"Well-fed slaves grow lazy and uppity," he said again and again in warning to us.

I am telling you this so that you may understand slavery and how it affected slave and master.

Now the good Father crossed the room and caught me by my collar. "Where were you?" he demanded to know, and his blue eyes glowered like a vulture's.

How could I lie to a priest of God?

Aunt Rebekah would not look at me. I was responsible for my own words. Water in the bucket swooshed against the sides. I stared at the water.

"Father, I went to the well." Half-true, I thought.

"Did you carry food out to the field slaves?"

That question was direct. "Father," I said, "we have had no food." Avoiding his eyes, I stared at water in the bucket. "I'm sorely hungry, Father." Avoiding the truth with the truth.

Miss Emily Fitzpatrick pushed open the kitchen door. She held out a cut-glass water pitcher. It was empty.

Aunt Rebekah clasped her hands. "Yes, Miss Emily," she said, smiling now, "I sent Moses for the water."

With a scowl Father Fitzpatrick turned to stare at his sister. She simply held out the crystal pitcher. That pitcher hadn't been empty five minutes before. Not even if she had filled all the glasses on the table would the pitcher be empty. Miss Emily must have opened the refectory window and poured the water out. That proved that she was in sympathy with us.

Once I heard her ask her brother, "Dennis, how can

you face God on your altar, when you know you're starving slaves on your rice lands?"

You must understand that there were many white people aware of the human misery of slavery. That is why I have begun my account five long days before that clipper set sail for Isle à Vache. You must understand the consequences of slavery.

I think Father Fitzpatrick felt foolish, and that was dangerous. He did not like to be caught wrong. A tall man, he put his hands behind his back, his long black cassock pulled across his round protruding belly, and he strode back into the refectory. I filled the pitcher.

As I carried it to the table, I begged God's forgiveness on my lying lips. I had not told Father the full truth, but I hadn't told a lie, either. Thinking for myself was so confusing.

After dinner Miss Emily retired to her bedroom with a candle. The priests and old Mr. Fitzpatrick lit cigars stinky enough to make a frog croak, and sat in deep upholstered chairs in the parlor.

I leaped to clear the table and wash dishes. Poor Aunt Rebekah laid her ponderous body on a raised bench behind the wood-burning stove. The year before, Porter and I had built that crude bench in that warm, almost-hidden spot so that she might rest while preparing Father's repasts. Her pain was so great, sometimes she could barely stand.

From time to time I heard her groan. Neither of us dared discuss the field slaves's food. Father Fitzpatrick had a way of listening by the door. So disturbed was I that I forgot to eat!

After sweeping and mopping, I tiptoed toward my room. Aunt Rebekah whispered, "Moses."

I returned and knelt by her. Her breathing was harsh and windy that night, and there was a rattle in her chest.

"Christmas morn," she said, "Mr. Dawson be sailing up to visit his daughter in Washington. Go with him. Don't come back."

I shook my head no. "I have to help you with meals, Aunt Rebekah. Father has company, remember? And it's Christmas Day!"

She squeezed my arm. "Go, child, go while you can. Father is fixing to sell some of you to live down South. Go, Moses."

I patted her fleshy arm and kissed her forehead. Her head turned. Her eyes rolled back showing white. I hadn't seen the likes of that before, but I threw her cloak over her. Ofttimes she slept all night behind the warm stove.

By my cot in the pantry where I slept, I heard Father's voice. I had started to undress in the frosty winter darkness, but I stopped and crept toward the parlor, to a place where I could hear better. First lying then being deceitful. What was I coming to?

". . . selling five of them," I heard Father say. "Moses among them. He's tall for his age. I'll get seven or eight hundred for him."

Seven or eight hundred was a goodly sum for a boy. Since the war, grown men sold for little more than that!

"But Dennis," said another priest, "I suspect Lincoln will free even our slaves in a few months. Why not let them finish out their service here? For the salvation of their souls, man!"

"Will they be purchased where they can practice their faith?" asked the second priest. I didn't know their names. They were Sulpicians from Baltimore, I believe. They too owned slaves.

"St. Mary's needs the money," said Father Fitzpatrick. "The rectory roof leaks in two places."

I had heard enough. Aunt Rebekah was right about his plans for me, but the other slaves he wanted to sell were long gone. I felt indignation. How could Father sell me like any farm animal? I loved him. He had taught me from the time I was five or six years old. Surely I was more than a slave to him?

I served him from early morning, when I carried in his coffee, heated his bathwater, filled the tub, scrubbed his back, and laid out his clothes. At midday I cleaned his rooms, served his meals, cleared his table, and washed his clothes with Rebekah's help. Evenings I lit his stinky cigars, brought his slippers and ran his errands. I was a house slave-boy. How could he sell me like any ordinary field slave?

Indignation and rage swept over me like storm waters from the bay. Aunt Rebekah was right. I ran back to tell her.

As soon as I stepped into the kitchen I knew something had happened. I stood listening. Aunt Rebekah was silent, terribly silent. Her windy breath no longer rattled. Tears washed my cheeks before I reached her. She was dead. I knelt and rested my head upon her warm, soft breasts.

On Father's rice lands Aunt Rebekah was the one who laid the dead to rest. Time and again I had washed dead bodies with her, reaching where she couldn't reach. But now I would not bathe Aunt Rebekah. I pulled her black cloak off and wiped her face and arms. To set her eyelids closed, I placed teaspoons over her eyes.

Her legs I laid straight, and I tied her feet together upright. I folded her warm, fleshy arms upon her chest. I put blocks of firewood on either side to hold her head face up.

Then I stood trembling in silent teary sobs. Now I had no one in the world. Although I attended Mass with field slaves, they were jealous of me, and I was terrified of them. Aunt Rebekah had been my bridge to them. Now she was gone.

And the good Father? Ordinarily I would have run sobbing to him. But now I knew him as Aunt Rebekah had tried to show me. He was a slave owner: one who bought, worked, and sold slaves. A slave owner just like all the rest of them.

Once in a pamphlet I read what our most-esteemed Frederick Douglass said about the corruption of owning slaves. Then I thought it was false and sinful. Now I knew it was true: Owning human persons as slaves corrupts the spirits of owners as well as deforming the spirits and abusing the bodies of slaves. That must be why the good Father was selling me. He was corrupted, notwithstanding his being a priest!

I must run and seek my fortune elsewhere, I thought. But I was angry. I wanted to call lightning down to burn the church. I had always been obedient to Father. Now I wanted to scream and yell at him: "You're no better than any of them. You buy and sell and starve and order whippings of human beings whom God loves!" Yet, what could I do?

I ran silently to pack a change of clothes and I bundled them in Aunt Rebekah's cloak. This bundle and my own cloak I set in the churchyard at a distance. When I slipped back inside, I heard Father and the other men go up to bed.

Then I went and robbed the altar of St. Mary's of the Sea. I lugged the huge gold crucifix and its stand from the altar and set it at the end of the bench at Aunt Rebekah's head. A smaller gold cross with diamonds I laid on her breast. I placed ten fat candles set in marble-and-gold candlesticks on each side of her body. After I lit the twenty candles, the sweet smell of melting beeswax quickly filled the small kitchen. All the treasures of St. Mary's surrounded her. Gold, diamonds, and the glorious flickering candlelight were fitting for a great woman.

I knelt and prayed an Our Father, noting painfully the ". . . forgive us our trespasses as we forgive those who trespass against us." It caught in my throat like a hook in a catfish mouth.

In half an hour I was at the dock where Mr. Dawson kept his boat. I boarded easily and found an empty box meant for fishing tackle and nets and corks. In the box I lay on Aunt Rebekah's cloak and covered myself with my cloak. I propped the lid open with two corks. And then I wept again.

I heard the boat dip as two others jumped aboard that cold, dark Christmas Eve night. An infant whimpered. I was not alone, but what would the morrow hold for me?

That Christmas morning was sparkling clear. No snowflakes lingered on the grass, and sunlight warmed the air. Mr. Dawson was a kindly fisherman from our eastern Potomac shore. He boarded with armfuls of packages— probably gifts for his grandchildren.

His sail was stored in a canvas bag. He ran the fasteners up the tract on the mast, heaved down the halyard, and hoisted the mainsail. The Potomac River was fairly calm, but his sails caught a light wind.

When we were far from either shore of the river, he laid out sliced ham and placed rolls and coffee on a tablecloth. Peering from my fishing tackle box, I saw that he was alone, and that the food was more than he could ever eat. Why had he laid it there?

The smell of warm ham teased my nostrils. When Mr. Dawson settled at the helm to steer the boat, I saw a black man dressed in tattered clothes slip toward the food, take some, and disappear. Likewise, a woman wearing rags and carrying an infant took food and hid. Lifting the lid of my box, I too crawled over, grabbed a soft roll, and stuck juicy warm ham inside. I drank from the cup of lukewarm coffee, and refilled the cup. Back into the box I climbed and pulled the lid shut.

As I ate curled inside, I remembered that I hadn't eaten on Christmas Eve. In haste I had stored the lamb and other victuals to cool outside. After Aunt Rebekah's death I couldn't eat. Now my innards reminded me that I was hungry.

Wolfing down the juicy ham and soft bread, I thought about my position in life. I couldn't speak the language of ordinary slaves, slaves like those uneducated ragged people hiding with me on the sailboat. My upbringing had been different.

Every day I bathed and dressed well. At breakfast I read aloud from the Maryland newspapers to Father Fitzpatrick. I penned his letters and wrote reports to his bishop. I even felt superior to crude white fishermen like Mr. Dawson.

But no more. Now I was a runaway slave like any other. I felt branded by this deep brown skin, these broad nostrils, and these thick lips. I felt ashamed to be a Negro. I had let the good Father make me feel superior to his field slaves. Now I felt more alone than ever.

After the other slaves ate again, I took a larger chunk of ham and three rolls of bread. I wrapped the food to keep and fell asleep, embarrassed to be stealing food and hiding in a box.

Some hours later, when Mr. Dawson hailed a man at the Washington wharf, I peeked from the lid of my box, then dropped it as I heard him lower the sails. Later I looked again. His back was turned, and I watched the other two slaves jump to the dock and run. Mr. Dawson simply raised his head a little and smiled. Now I knew how some slaves escaped Maryland. I wasn't so bold.

I couldn't get out of my box. Every time I raised the lid, I was frightened by a sound or a voice. As I waited, homesickness dragged me to drown in sadness. I was homesick for St. Mary's, which was never really home; for a man I called the "good Father," who was not my father; and for a woman I called Aunt Rebekah, who was not my aunt.

But to me, she had been everything. She had raised me from two or three years of age, when my mother had died of malaria. And Aunt Rebekah had tried to set balance to what the good Father ordered me to do and say.

With deep shame I remembered how Father Fitzpatrick had instructed me to listen in the rice lands.

"Moses," he had said, "help me with these savage field slaves. They're different from you. Tell me what they're saying about me. Be a good boy now, and listen well."

Aunt Rebekah taught me better.

"Moses," she had said, "you just a little boy, but don't you believe what that Father say. You told on Mary, her complaint of being mighty hungry. And Father took her food away for two days. And now 'cause you tattled, the overseer gonna beat Cephas for stealing chicken eggs."

I wanted to tell her that Cephas was a savage, and that beatings didn't hurt him. That's what Father told me. But she made me watch the overseer's whip lash flesh from Cephas's shoulders and back. Cephas was in pain. I flinched with each blow and decided that there were two opposite versions of life: the good Father's and Aunt Rebekah's.

From that day forth I told Father nothing important.

He pressed me, but I had a selective memory. Aunt Rebekah taught me how to make quick judgments, and I would need that now that I was alone in the world seeking my fortune.

I watched Mr. Dawson cast anchor from the bow, tie up to the wharf, and leave. Other boats sailed in for Christmas. In the evening, when at last the wharf was quiet, I climbed out of the box. I combed my hair and smoothed wrinkles from my clothes. After I donned my cloak, I tied my small bundle around my waist. But I couldn't leave without thanking Mr. Dawson.

I tore paper from a notebook in the stern, and wrote him. Thank you, Mr. Dawson. Merry Christmas.

I dared not sign my name. And what was my name now that I had left Father Fitzpatrick? My identity had been as his slave, and I wasn't the good Father's slave anymore.

I decided to tell Mr. Dawson about Aunt Rebekah because they had been friends, as close as a slave woman and a white fisherman could be. He had brought her select fish and crabs and clams to cook for Father, and passed messages along to her friends. I added to my note the following: Aunt Rebekah of Father Fitzpatrick died Christmas morning of tumors.

Jumping onto the dock, I climbed over the gate. Seafood markets along the wharf were all closed for the holiday. No piles of fish with glassy staring eyes and silvery scales were on display outside the stores. No men stood in boots and bloody aprons cleaning fish. In shop after shop, no laughing sellers, no haggling buyers. I had never seen the wharf this silent, empty, cold. It made me feel more lonely than ever. That night I slept inside a shop. The next morning, a runaway slave, a lonely boy, I walked into downtown Washington, D.C.

I strolled the city streets. Carriages bedecked with cheerful ribbons and tinkling Christmas bells passed me. I loved the bells, and thought of the mellow bells of St. Mary's of the Sea. Well-cared-for horses daintily lifted hooves and snorted greetings.

As I stared at the horses, it seemed people cared better for their horses than for their slaves. Would they starve horses to punish them?

Across Washington I walked, along M Street to Connecticut Avenue. There around noon a troop of bedraggled soldiers wearing Union blues and bloody red bandages stumbled rather than marched past me. I suspected that they were seeking hospital care.

Horse-drawn wagons passed with men lying on stretchers and looking out the back. They were part of the forlorn parade.

As a group of wounded soldiers passed, I spied a man standing across the avenue. Thin and gaunt of face, he was tall and well dressed. A plump, short woman dressed in black clung to his arm. He had bushy black eyebrows and beard, piercing brown eyes, swarthy skin. Yes, it was our most excellent president, Mr. Abraham Lincoln.

After seeing pictures, I couldn't miss him. Yet only slowly did it dawn on me that I stood a mere twenty or so feet from the man Aunt Rebekah called Father Abraham, the Great Liberator. He was a lawyer, concerned about justice, an emancipator.

After a two-wheel buggy passed, I boldly crossed the

street before our most honorable president could leave. He stood sadly watching the last of the wounded stragglers, but turned as I walked near. So bold was I that I made my approach without knowing what I would say. Two men behind Mr. Lincoln watched me.

The president's eyes seemed moist. I do believe that he was close to weeping. His awful responsibility for ordering soldiers to war crept into my mind. He must feel pain and guilt, I thought. I recognized the suffering in his eyes, and so I extended the hand of a fourteen-year-old. I hoped he saw understanding of his pain visible in my eyes.

He took my hand graciously. I had heard that he shook hands with Frederick Douglass and other colored leaders.

"Mr. President, we are most appreciative of emancipation," I said in a clear loud voice. Father Fitzpatrick had never allowed me to mumble. I could be grateful for that.

I had spoken for Aunt Rebekah and for over four million slaves in rebel states. I, Moses of Father Fitzpatrick!

Mr. Lincoln nodded. Sadly, it seemed. I had read of the criticism he had received from the cabinet and Congress as a result of his Emancipation Proclamation. Aunt Rebekah said ofttimes the right path is a lonely one. The president turned and, putting hands behind his black frock coat, strode away. His round-faced wife swished long skirts as she walked beside him.

That gives me the hope that these words about Cow Island suffering, these descriptions of the degradation done by slavery to slaves and owners, will one day be read by no less than our President Lincoln. I am sure he will remember me. After all, Christmas was only five months ago as I begin this writing.

And that was how I decided to change my slave name of Moses of Father Fitzpatrick to a free boy's name: Moses Lincoln. Moses Lincoln alone in the world.

4

The next day a fishmonger at the Washington wharf offered me work. "Moses," Mr. Smith said, "I don't suppose you can clean fish in those fancy clothes?"

"You'll find me a good worker," I said. I changed into work clothes I had brought and began cleaning fish beside him. From many trips for Aunt Rebekah, I was well known at the wharves.

"Since I'm free now," I told him, "I should get paid."

He laughed. "You've got soft hands and lying lazy ways. What makes you think you deserve pay? I've a mind to shackle you and send you back to that priest down the river."

I swallowed my ire. "I think you'll pay me, sir, because you need my help." How high-minded could he be? There was work enough for three, and him being only one, I was most serviceable. Besides, pay for a free boy's work was a matter of justice.

"Well," and he looked around. "My Jim hasn't come in for two days. I suppose he's still drunk from Christmas wine."

"Yes, sir." Mr. Smith didn't know it, but I had been

sleeping in the back of his shop for two days. I suppose, had he known, he would have charged me for the room!

For supper he tossed me a can of Van Camp's pork and beans. I had never seen canned food not in jars. Union soldiers carried cans on battlefields. For breakfast I drank Bordens canned milk. How thick and creamy it tasted. Real hunger and I had been unfamiliar, but we were introduced during those days after Christmas. With shame I had eaten from warm garbage.

On the third day after my departure I heard Father Fitzpatrick's angry voice calling my name at the dock. I began to tremble. I hadn't thought that he would seek me. Did he care after all? The sound of his voice stirred tender feelings. I was so lonely for St. Mary's of the Sea; I yearned to run, to kneel at the good Father's feet, to beg his pardon now that he had come after me. But, no, I thought. No, no, no!

Memory of Aunt Rebekah stopped me. Christmas Eve she had prayed for my freedom. Aunt Rebekah had wanted me to make a good life for myself, and I would. I must not give in to slave feelings. Fighting the weakness of my heart, I fumbled for the sword of courage in my head.

I dropped my fish knife and ripped off my bloody apron. Everyone along the wharf knew where I was working. I grabbed a loaf of bread and a short workingman's jacket Jim had left. I ran, leaving my bundle. Regrettably I left Rebekah's dear cloak that had covered me in the frosty December nights.

I ran wildly along the wharf, passing familiar shops. If I darted into another shop, that owner might turn me over to Father. I could jump onto a fishing boat, but where would it take me? I must needs leave the wharf where I was known, and seek my fortune elsewhere.

At the end of the wharf stood a wagon full of wooden barrels. I decided to hide there. Climbing up, I squeezed among the barrels and had just made room for myself when the team of horses began clip-clopping away. Good. The horses were leaving the wharf. Those barrels smelled sharp and sour. I suspected they held sauerkraut or pickles, but I wasn't hungry enough to try opening one.

Mr. Smith hadn't paid me and I was penniless, but none the worse for it. I had never had a penny of my own. It's hard to miss being rich when you've always been poor. And I had taken a loaf of bread.

The wagon driver stopped at several taverns. After the third tavern he began singing sea ditties. I leaned back and stared up.

Bleak December skies lit bare limbs of skeletal trees. The trees were like black souls clawing for blue heaven. Sometimes, I admit, I wondered why God allowed so much suffering. But my mind knew right from wrong at last. I decided Aunt Rebekah's understanding of life was closer to truth than the good Father's version. And I had begun to think about justice.

The slave's main comfort was in knowing that after this life there was some justice, heaven for those who helped others. If any soul deserved heaven, Aunt Rebekah did. She rested at long last. At that moment, I felt so lonely and fearful that I wept, not for Aunt Rebekah, but for myself.

What would I do with my life now? Aunt Rebekah had always whispered, "Moses, you a smart boy. You learned reading and writing. Ain't many of our brethren got your talents."

Now, I wondered, how could I use those talents?

That wagon driver now dozed as his horses clip-clopped surely on a path out New York Avenue in Washington. Toward evening he stopped, fed and watered his horses, and put them up in a barn.

He threw chains over his barrels, and locked them securely. I barely missed being clunked on the head by a chain. I was most pleased at not being hit, as I needed all my wits. When he went to his lodging, I stretched, jumped down, and relieved myself outside the wagon. Chewing my dry bread, I strolled in the woods until I heard someone whistle. Then I crept forward on the soft ground.

A tall, muscular black man stood, hair graying, hand on an oak's trunk. He was staring straight at me. His lips were parted, his head slightly tilted. He was dressed fairly well in a black broadcloth suit, and carried a leather pouch tucked under his arm with its strap over one shoulder.

I froze, held my breath. Still he stared. I raised my hand and moved it slowly through the air in an arc. The man's stare never changed. When a bird murmured, he moved his head slightly toward the sound. Now I knew that the man was utterly blind, blinder than a headless chicken.

I shuffled my feet, and he startled. Stepping forward I said, "Good evening, sir."

From a puzzled stare, he broke into a servile grin. "Young master," he said, "I be looking for Solomon's Inn. And thank you kindly, young master."

I laughed. From my way of speaking, he took me for a

white boy. To a slave all white people are masters. That dawned painfully at that moment.

"Good sir, I am of African descent like yourself, and earth brown to prove it. Forgive my speech." Walking up, I shook his hand. "My name is Moses."

"Goshen here, and pleased to make your acquaintance." Although his hair was graying, he was nimble moving and acted young. Perchance this Goshen was in middle thirties in age.

He grasped my arm with one hand, squeezed my shoulder with the other. I sensed that he was judging my size. "Do you have any food, Moses?" he asked softly.

Together we finished my loaf of bread. He carried a tin cup in his pouch, and we drank water from a nearby stream.

"I am going to Annapolis," he said. "Or anywhere else a blind free man can work. I've ofttimes laid brick with a helper, I've loaded ships in a work line." His speech had changed to match mine. He seemed to have been a house slave too.

Mentioning to the wagon, I said, "You are welcome to squeeze in beside me there. The address written on the side says Annapolis, Maryland, although the driver is taking a month of Sundays to arrive."

He almost leaped from the log where we were sitting. "You can read, Moses?"

"Yes, sir." I told him how Father Dennis Fitzpatrick taught me to read and write for him, albeit against the law.

He pulled three letters from his pouch. It was the dark of the moon that night, but the next morning in the wagon I read him letters from his mother in Louisiana. Her letters were mostly news of family and friends, both freemen and slaves.

Reading a mother's letters made me feel as lonely as an empty sky at dawn. In truth, I was a motherless child. What would my mother write to me? What would Rebekah have someone write to me? It gave me pause. Nonetheless I believed that Aunt Rebekah would have been pleased with my freedom.

Goshen's mother had mailed the letters to a Catholic church in Baltimore. Goshen was Catholic like myself.

At noon our wagon stopped in Annapolis by the sparkling blue Chesapeake Bay. Bustling men and boys rolled cargo in wheelbarrows, hauled crates on shoulders, and dragged nets full of fishes. Amid the activity on the wooden walks, Goshen and I crawled off the wagon still unbeknownst to the driver.

With Goshen's hand on my shoulder, I wandered in a daze, astonished at the great ships and bustling activity. The day was clear, sunny, and cold. I could see where sky blue matched sea blue and hugged the earth with tender light.

Annapolis had old square-rigged ships from Europe, and some new ships with steam power. There were old-style brigantines and clipper ships. Blind Goshen taught me about them, gave them names. By now I knew, this was in truth, no ordinary man. His brilliance shone like a diamond.

"Tell me what you see, Moses?" asked Goshen as we strolled the docks, trying to stay out of the way of darting sailors.

I described some small sails. "Those are jibs," he said.

Apparently he had worked ships and wharves before he became blind.

"Do you see any pretty maidens? Any tavern wenches? Describe them to me!" he asked.

"There's one," I said.

"Yes, yes?"

"She's thick as a cistern, has white hair like seaweed at high tide, and laughs like a sick crow. Hear her voice there?"

Goshen groaned and chuckled. I described a ship next.

"Aye," he said, "the bluff-bowed square-bottom ships are good for cargo." He sighed. "Ofttimes slaves as cargo, my boy. Our great-grandparents were brought to these United States on those boats. 'Twas called the 'Blackbird trade' in code. There was an opium trade too."

"What's opium?" I asked.

"Something to avoid. Living death," he said. "It's a thickened paste made of poppies, flowers of the East. The poppy juice dulls the mind and deadens the heart."

It was the twenty-ninth of December that day. Goshen kept a firm grip on my shoulder. I realized that, like it or not, I was not alone anymore. All night he had held to my foot, and by day his clasp made me aware that he was not going to let me slip away. I wondered if Aunt Rebekah had ordered him for me? Was he a gift of Christmas angels?

We had walked in silence for two hundred feet or more when Goshen pointed. "And that ship?"

I wondered what sounds let him know a ship was there.

"It's long and narrow," I told him. "Has a sharp-pointed bow and stern. . . ."

"A Baltimore clipper," he said. "Now that's a ship!

Shaped for speed like a fish. The square-bow ships make three to four knots speed, but the clippers sail nine to ten knots. American ships—clippers—built hereabouts in Virginia or Maryland. Of course," he added, "steam ships are faster still."

"Three men in a long boat from the clipper are rowing to the dock," I told Goshen. "They're waving to us."

"Maybe we can get a job on board, Moses!"

I stared at Goshen. How could this blind man work? However, I needed money to begin my life as a free person.

An hour later, alongside thirty or more coloreds recruited on the wharf for work, Goshen and I were aboard that Baltimore clipper.

"**W**elcome aboard," called a daintily dressed gentleman that first afternoon on the clipper. The thick gold fob to his watch glittered in chilly December sunshine, and he wore a green silk kerchief about his neck. His name was Mr. Forbes, and he introduced a Mr. Tuckerman, who stood behind him staring at us and twitching. In the distance church bells rang out the noon Angelus prayer, and the anchored ship swung back and forth with the Chesapeake Bay.

Five white men and a boy stood above us on the quarterdeck at the mizzenmast. Naturally I noticed the boy. He was dressed as a sailor in tight pants, jacket, and sailor cap, but his clothes were faded and in shreds. He seemed quite curious about us blacks, standing near the railing and staring at me in particular. He seemed eager to speak with me. We were about the same size, but I was tall for my age. I suspected he was older, perchance seventeen.

Mr. Forbes said, "You are part of a new colonization plan. Governor Kock here"—Mr. Forbes pointed to a blue-eyed man, fairly young, with unruly brown hair sticking out under a black derby; through the railings I noticed shiny

black walking shoes and smart gray spats at his ank
"Governor Kock," he went on, "has a lease for land in l____, __
on Isle à Vache."

Governor Kock leaned over the rail and waved at us.
He seemed friendly as he glanced from face to face, turning
to walk around the quarterdeck to wave to coloreds on the
other side. He walked like a Maryland politician seeking
votes.

"Henceforth," said Mr. Forbes, "you'll work the land
and earn money. Money for buying farms. Isle à Vache will
be your own country from this day forth."

"Own country?" someone whispered. "Us have our own
country right here."

"When we git to eat?" The man who asked stooped as
if to hide in the crowd. I thought he was most ungrateful.
Mr. Forbes was explaining where we were going, and already
this man was asking for food.

Governor Kock raised a hand. "We'll have food as we
promised. Our suppliers are late." He spoke with a heavy
German accent.

"But we've been here a week, boss," a muffled voice
said. A week? No food? Goshen's grip on my shoulder tightened.

I glanced back and looked around. The colored people
were a sad lot for the most part. Dressed in tattered clothing, they stood shoulder to shoulder, shivering and crowded
on the deck. I supposed they had come up from below deck
for the announcement. Followed by Goshen, I backed away.
I elbowed my way through the crowd and stared below deck,
where black men and women were as crowded as above.

People standing at the ladder top were passing word along to those below.

They whispered: "Still no food. Say supply late." My God, I thought, there are hundreds of people here.

At the words, the people below barely breathed a sigh. Poor people, I thought. As slaves they were fearful of complaining. And now on this boat they are still afraid. They? I was setting myself apart. I myself hadn't been able to ask questions or complain, either. Father had called slaves obstinate or uppity if they didn't obey immediately.

"What is it, Moz?" asked Goshen. I wove a path farther through the crowd, all the way to the pointed bow, where there were people only on one side of us.

The bow had a huge wooden carving of a three-horned ram. Two horns curved back. One long horn stuck out three yards straight ahead. Surely this was an animal of medieval fantasy? It looked as if it belonged in one of those tapestries pictured in the good Father's books. Notwithstanding the unusual third horn, it was a handsome statue.

Since we had moved away from the white men, I whispered: "Some of them haven't eaten. Below deck is crowded with men, women, and infants that I could hear crying."

Goshen nodded. "I smelled disease down there. Loose bowels and fever." He paused. "Moz, we'll leave this little colonization plan," he said. "Look for a boat to shore."

I hated to be called Moz. My name was Moses.

From the corner of my eye I spied the captain readying a rowboat for Messieurs Forbes and Tuckerman.

"Goshen, there's a boat to go ashore. We'll stand here by this ladder and ask."

An older man at my elbow said, "They ain't letting none of us go. Yesterday they hauled three back in nets."

"Hauled back?" Goshen said.

"They had jumped overboard," a young man beside us said. "Mr. Kock there ordered nets set out to catch any jumping off. He's getting fifty dollars a head for us."

"What?" I said. "Are we being sold?" I felt indignant. "Father Fitzpatrick said he could get seven or eight hundred dollars for me," I said. "Fifty dollars is an insult."

Goshen shook me by the shoulder. "Moses, do you really measure your worth in money?" He moaned.

The young man shook his head. "They say President Lincoln want to get rid of us now that we free. They say white folks can't live alongside of us, or work alongside of us, neither."

A brisk breeze smarted on my face, but those words chilled me more. Surely President Lincoln was not involved in this colonization? He had shaken my hand!

My hands and feet were so cold they were as numb as a sleeping skeleton; however, my inside position with Goshen and others crowded around did give some small measure of warmth.

A young woman joined our circle within the crowd. She said, "We is better off slaves if they gotta send us away. My mama, and her mama, and her mama before her all borned in Virginia, and they sending me away to another country? Call 'eel ah wash'?"

"Isle à Vache," I said correcting her. "In French it means island of a cow. Cow Island."

People turned to look at me and passed word of what I

said. I felt embarrassed, but it was true. Father taught me Latin from the Mass and books, of course, and he taught me some French, and a little Spanish.

By now the movements of the ship were making me feel dizzy. The sea was different from the boat on the Potomac River. The river was fairly smooth, but here waves slapped the ship and we rose and fell on the water.

"I be Cassius," said the older man, extending his hand. "And this be my son, Simeon. We wanna work the land. Own a farm. But if Mr. Kock don't feed us soon. . . ."

The young woman was Sarah. "I can work," she said. "But they tricked me aboard this here boat. I ain't sure I wanna go to no Cow Island."

Several people listening to us grunted in agreement. A man whispered: "Tricked me too. Told me I'd have my own farm for cotton. Didn't say nothing about Hayti or no island."

Goshen whispered, "What does she look like?" He had stooped by my ear.

"Who?"

"Sarah! Who are you concerned with?"

"Oh. Why must needs you know?" I was teasing him.

He pinched my arm.

"Sarah," I said so she couldn't hear, "is slender, has sandy brown eyes, even pearly teeth, and rich, dark-brown skin. Her hair is long, thick and kinky. It's parted in the middle and rolled into two buns, one over each ear."

Goshen sighed and swallowed. I noticed his Adam's apple slide up and down. "But we're leaving, remember?" I told him.

Goshen could hear heeled shoes coming to the side of the boat. "Be ready," he whispered.

I saw the captain fold his arms. Two sailors held rifles. Other sailors opened a path and held us back with arms spread. Nevertheless, I worked my way toward the railing, Goshen right behind me. Cassius and his son were watching. With thumb up, Sarah gestured for us to try.

Mr. Forbes spoke loudly as he click-clacked his heels toward us on the wooden deck. "Bernard," he said over his shoulder to Mr. Kock, "if you succeed at this colony, our president and Congress will praise and reward you. We'll send back in the rowboat any blacks we find loitering on the wharf. And best of luck to you!"

"I am most grateful," Mr. Kock said, "but we're full now. I have more than four hundred head of coloreds for the trip."

Mr. Tuckerman held a kerchief to his nose as he drew near. I remembered that I hadn't had a bath lately. Mr. Tuckerman waved his kerchief and said:

"You'll lose some. There are five dead bodies below deck already, and some young woman is dying on the other side. You'll need quinine for malaria on Hayti. In fact, you'll lose quite a few of these blacks from starvation and dysentery. Crowd them on. Remember the money. You get paid by the head leaving the States. Crowd them on."

A chill stiffened my spine. After hearing those words I felt ill. Goshen loosened and tightened his grip.

A sailor opened the gate to a ladder leading down to the rowboat. Following two sailors, Messieurs Forbes and Tuckerman climbed down the rope ladder, still calling good wishes.

When the moment came, Goshen and I tried to leap off. A sailor caught me by the heels. Another sailor struck Goshen on the head and pulled him back from the rail. Sarah screamed for us.

"We don't want your old Cow Island!" she yelled. "Leave us go home to our United States of America. I is a Virginian. I been borned in Virginia, and I wanna die in Virginia!"

Someone threw me down and struck me twice in the stomach with the butt of a rifle. From the deck I was clawing for Goshen. I was afraid they might get rid of him or kill him if they knew he was blind.

Mr. Kock gave orders to the sailors. His friendly-sounding voice seemed like poisoned syrup. "Take the woman and these two into my office."

My stomach pained like rippling lightning in a thunderstorm. I walked bent over clutching my innards. Goshen seemed dazed. Dragged along, Sarah held hands on hips in defiance. We were doomed, I thought.

My heart tolled like funeral bells at St. Mary's of the Sea.

6

I pulled Goshen to sit beside me on the floor of Mr. Kock's small bunkroom-office. It was warm inside. Our backs were against a pinewood cabinet. A lower cabinet supported a bunk, and a brass spittoon shone in light from the portholes. By then it was midafternoon. Sarah sat in the middle of the floor.

A desk built into the bunkroom wall had a sign which read:

BERNARD KOCK
GOVERNOR
ISLE À VACHE

It was well printed in gold on black. At St. Mary's we had such a sign for hours of Mass and Confessions. This sign looked as if the gold ink were still wet.

When everything seemed quiet outside, Sarah asked, "You gentlemen bring any food with you?"

"No," I whispered, bent over in pain.

Goshen nodded, but said, "They may take this away from me. Moz, hide this." He handed me what felt like coins in a tiny pouch. I folded it in my palm. Then he opened his shirt.

He gave Sarah a chunk of bread, my bread from the night before. "It's our last piece," he told me. I was surprised. Henceforth I would remember that. Always eat some, hide some.

I spied a brass navy button under the cabinet and I slipped it in with the coins. I once had a button collection, but the good Father said it was frivolous to collect worldly things of no value. I was no longer slave to Father Fitzpatrick. I would start another collection that the good Father couldn't throw away.

Sarah chewed the dry bread hungrily. "I been on board some three days," she said. "They given us a cup of water in the morning and another in the evening. Got half a yam the first day, ain't got no food since then, none of us. Say we have us some sea biscuits once we set sail."

I groaned. If we didn't die from drowning, we might die from starvation. I looked at Goshen. "How do you feel?"

He held his head. "My head pounds like waves in a storm. Besides that I'm fair to middling. And you?"

"They struck me in the stomach. I think a rib is cracked. The pain is awful." I wondered, Did my Aunt Rebekah have pain like this? Was this what the other slaves felt when they were whipped?

When she heard footsteps, Sarah sidled over to me. We huddled, and I could barely keep from moaning.

"Blighty right, Mr. Kock," we heard the captain say outside the door, "they ain't about to deliver food till you pay them."

"Fools!" said Kock. "I'm good for twenty thousand dollars, fifty dollars a head, I tell you."

"Aye, sire, but you ain't in possession o' that money now."

"No," Mr. Kock said more softly. "It's to my credit. A year ago Congress set aside more than half a million dollars for Lincoln's colonization plans. As soon as they see how successful this colony is, they'll pay me. I have a contract."

"Well, Governor," the captain said, "I ain't got no clearance to pull anchor. These here people can't work on your colony if they ain't fed. And whereabouts is your farm tools?"

"Captain, no need to worry. It's only a little misunderstanding. Mr. Forbes may send food back on the rowboat, and we'll be cleared to leave in no time. You'll see." Mr. Kock chuckled as if there were a joke between them.

The captain cleared his throat. "Governor, could I see that there contract?"

"Why certainly, my Captain. Perchance this evening after supper?"

"Blighty right now, Governor!"

"Oh. Well. Are you doubting me? You just spoke with Mr. Forbes and Mr. Tuckerman. They're from New York and they're backing me. Mr. Leonard W. Jerome and Mr. Henry J. Raymond are also interested parties."

Mr. Kock turned the knob and opened the door. Now we could see them. He said, "No less than President Abraham Lincoln himself wants these unfortunate people in a climate congenial to them. Besides, they're hoping deportation will keep the newly freed slaves out of the North."

"The contract, Governor. If this here trip ain't legal, me and my sailors will see eye to eye with trouble. And after, it'll take a month to scrub down this ship. My ship ain't built to carry this many people, and they're suffering to boot."

"Oh, Captain, don't be concerned. They're used to being hungry and crowded."

The captain yelled, "They're human, ain't they?"

"The contract, sir," said Mr. Kock. "I'll get it right away. Then you'll see." Governor Kock opened the door fully and came in with a cheerful smile. If I hadn't heard the conversation outside the door, I would have thought he had just eaten apple pie with butter crust.

Barely giving us a glance, he tore through boxes, searching. The captain stood in the doorway. His arms were folded and his pock-marked face wore a frown. He was small but muscular, and his balding pattern was like the tonsure of a Capuchin monk. I read sympathy in his glance; then he looked away from us.

Finally Governor Kock pulled out a sheet of paper. Removing his derby, he wiped his brow with the back of his hand.

"Yes, Captain," he said. "Here's my contract with no less than President Abraham Lincoln and the Congress of these United States. You'll notice it's dated 31 December 1862. We're ready in just one year, almost to the day."

He waved the contract under the captain's nose, but the captain caught it. He stepped into the bunkroom. As the passageway was dark, he read by light coming in the porthole.

"It's all legal," said Kock, "scriven by a government

lawyer. People are right to be careful when setting sail for new creative policies." He laughed and patted the captain on the back. "I approve of your prudence, Captain."

I think Governor Kock thought the captain might be illiterate, or read poorly. In Kock I smelled a person Father Fitzpatrick would call a "skunk wearing baby's breath."

"Governor Kock," the captain said, "this here contract ain't worth the ink it's writ with."

"Oh, sir, if you're doubting—"

The captain raised his hand. "No, I read for myself when the U.S. Congress set up money for colonies of new-freed slaves, but this here contract don't say nothing. There's no U.S. seal. Why, you could've writ this up and signed it yourself!"

"No seal? Well, that's right. First we have to prove ourselves. Establish a successful colony. Then that half million dollars will be mine. And you'll be paid generously, Captain. Generously. Haven't Mr. Forbes and Mr. Tuckerman given you your advance for the trip?"

Governor Kock was still smiling, although a bit weaker. He kept patting the captain's blue jacket sleeve.

Finally the captain snatched his arm away and handed the contract back. As the captain stepped out of the room, the ship's boy tapped on the open door and stood at a respectful distance.

"So?" asked the captain, who was standing in the walkway.

"Captain Lane, sir, we been cleared to leave, sir. They saying the waiting's cause of suffering, sir. We can sail at dawn."

I thought, that will be the thirtieth day of December, 1863. From a contract of thirty-first December 1862 it was a year short a day—if the governor's contract were valid.

"And food for these poor wretches?" asked the captain.

The ship's boy shook his head. Sun-bleached white hair flew like hay on a hayfork. In Maryland they called these people towheads. His eyes were pale gray, as if sunbleached too. "No food 'cepting the moldy sea biscuits, sir, and the mate says we need to take on more water. Our supplies low too, he says, sir."

Captain Lane, I now knew his name, shook a fist in the air. "These cussed blacks are in need of food. I'm not about to stand around and watch folks starve, even if they are black."

"Good for you, Captain," said Governor Kock. "I'm sure the suppliers will obey your orders."

Captain Lane gave Governor Kock a glance that would have lit a fire without kindling, and stomped out. The ship's boy bowed to Governor Kock and turned to go.

"Boy," Governor Kock said, "what's your name?" He smiled and beckoned him into the room. I thought the governor looked like a spider in its web waving for a fly.

"Jack, sir."

"Well, Jack," he said, "see that black boy there?" He pointed to me.

"Aye, sir."

"See what nice garments he's wearing? Well, he'll wear your clothes, and you get his new warm wool garments." He turned to me and shook his finger in my face.

"This is what you deserve for insurrection. I saw you lead this man to the railing. What's your name?"

Pained in heart and stomach, I could barely speak. No longer Moses of Father Fitzpatrick, I had planned to be Moses Lincoln for our president who was beloved of Aunt Rebekah. But President Lincoln wanted to send us away. Now I had to decide on a new name. What name? What Christian Catholic name?

"I am Moses Christmas." A timely name at least, I thought.

Kock pointed at Goshen. "Is this man blind?"

I raised my voice. "On deck just now he was struck on the head, sir. He hasn't been able to see since then." Oh, my deceitful tongue! But Aunt Rebekah would have approved. I had to keep Goshen safe, and I was growing freer and freer of the good Father.

"Take off your garments!"

Jack stripped easily. Due to pain, I could hardly straighten up, and I held fast to the coin purse Goshen had given me. Jack wore no underwear and he seemed delighted with mine, hugging them and grinning. His pantaloons, shirt, and jacket were better than they seemed. Hidden pockets were everywhere. One had sharp fishhooks. I hid the coins there.

Shredded layers of cloth were on the outside, but solid layers of cloth were underneath. It was almost as if he wore an old patched layer on the outside for sympathy, and whole well-woven cloth inside as a secret lining. The fit was perfect. We were the same size after all.

From undressing, I felt ill. I began to gag, and I pulled the brass spittoon to my side. My vomit was mixed with blood. Hand to mouth, Sarah screamed and stared at me as if I were a dying cow.

When it rained that night, I believe the skies were weeping for us poor misguided souls.

Our next days on the ship passed in misery. The beam of the clipper ship was about one-fifth of the length, and it tapered greatly at bow and stern. Besides people standing everywhere, there were dozens of crates, dozens of barrels, lines everywhere, and the raised quarterdeck. Many on board were seasick.

Three times a day Governor Kock made those in the ship's hold come up two at a time, and those on deck take a turn below. It was warmer below, but since people had diarrhea and were seasick, the stench there was unbearable.

Although there was a man who dared lead people in songs, I sank into silence at first. I only vomited blood the first two days, but Sarah kept watch over me like a big sister. Feelings of weakness, dizziness, and pain grew dull. I was hungry, huddled against the cold, and haunted by memories of beloved Aunt Rebekah. Above deck or below, we slept in a crouched upright position for lack of space.

A smiling Jack tried to be friendly, but whenever I saw him in my clothes, I grew hot in the face, and my teeth clenched.

From the first the people thought that I was bold because I had led Goshen in our attempt to escape. They whispered about me. Goshen spread word:

"Any of you with papers can get them read by Moses. He's a boy that can read and write."

I discovered that illiterate people like to carry writing. Those with papers or letters asked me to read for them. As the only person on board named Moses, it seemed I was thrust into a biblical-leader position. But I was only fourteen. I didn't desire to be anyone's leader.

By the fourth day, however, I was ready to rebel against Governor Kock's three-times-a-day decree. I told people: "Come up from the hold any time you need." Above, all were in agreement to go down and take their places. Thus fouling the hold and fainting among the weak was less frequent. Goshen and I, being strong, never fainted, and we helped clean up below deck.

Finally, to keep warm and sane, I began pushing through the crowd, helping people. Men and women showed gratitude.

"Thank you, Moses, for holding my baby girl while I been sick at the rail."

"Moses, tell my wife I be waiting at the mainmast."

"Moses, you eased my shoes off and my feets feel better. Thank you, son." Everyone knew my name.

Some days we sailed smoothly; other days we gently rocked on a becalmed ocean. And many days we stopped at ports along the coast of Virginia, the Carolinas, Georgia, and finally Florida. My only comfort was the growing warmth as we sailed south. Goods were taken on and off the ship, the crates and barrels that were always in our way. At each port hopes would fade that they could buy real food for us, more than the green sea biscuit we got each day; so small that it would fit into an eye, and so hard it cracked some people's teeth. Hunger and weakness were twin wolves at our throats.

Simeon, Cassius, Sarah, Goshen, and I stayed in touching space among the more than four hundred strangers.

Strangers: I listened to them. There were men who had worked as field hands, cooks, train porters, shoeshine boys, blacksmiths, bricklayers, carpenters. Men and women who had been born free, others who had been freed by President Lincoln's emancipation. Men and women in skin color from rich cow-milk yellow to rich delta-earth brown.

There were women who had worked as maids, cooks, shop clerks, laundresses, seamstresses, waitresses; however, men outnumbered women. That is to say, in the beginning, out of over four hundred of us, there were maybe fifteen or seventeen women.

These people, like myself, were used to work, and not given to the idleness of the crowded boat. I constantly proffered silent assistance—passing messages, freeing space above deck, going below myself—to all who required it. I was grateful to be accepted by them.

As I shuffled from above deck to below and across the deck, I learned the faces. I knew those who could still muster a smile, and those who could only stare blankly.

However, when I passed, people patted my shoulder. "Moses," some would say, "you born to do great things. You a smart boy."

Some who talked constantly helped keep the rest of us clear in the mind. Laughter followed every word. Their talk, hour after hour, went something like this:

"It be time for water soon."

"No. Won't. We just had morning water."

"Fool. Your mind is froze. It be afternoon."

"Think we'll eat today?"

"Mold on that biscuit is green like collards. Um, um!"

"I hear we having stew chicken today. Ha, ha!"

"Me thinks after I licked the green off, my little sea biscuit looked like a chicken thigh last night."

Governor Kock strutted among us like a rooster among hens. Captain Lane gave orders on how to address him. "You blighty right call that man mister. He ain't nobody's governor, and he ain't got no colony."

Governor, or rather, Mister Kock kept smiling. He was cheering us on as if it were a race we were running. He ate three times a day with the captain and mates; thus he could afford to feel cheerful.

Sarah pulled me and Goshen to the rail one day, after what I reckoned had been about a week and a half. "Moses," she said, "all five babies at the breast been died and thrown for shark food. Womens is weak, and so is mens."

Pained by her words, I leaned against Goshen. That morning I had watched a man's body, stripped of clothes and shoes, thrown overboard with no prayers or ceremony. Sailors tossed bodies that way almost every night. At St.

Mary's we buried our dogs with more respect. I had whispered in Latin:

"May perpetual light shine upon him, and may he rest in peace."

Now Sarah pointed to me. "Moses, peoples wants to know. How does this concern you?"

Me? I was only a fourteen-year-old boy. Besides, my side was aching, my stomach had a bruise as purple as day-old death, and I was dizzy from hunger. I closed my eyes in resentment.

Aunt Rebekah always gave me orders. Telling me to run away when I didn't want to. Why were there women, anyway? And what could I do?

Of course, Father Fitzpatrick had thought he could get seven or eight hundred dollars for me. And I was a house slave who could read and write. Never once under the whip, I had led a pampered life of relative luxury. Already I had created some freedom of movement on board ship above and below deck, and I had been of help to as many people as I could. Wasn't that enough even if I was named Moses after a great leader?

Food, food, food! People were starving to death. I knew that. Maybe it wasn't enough to do favors for people, not when they were starving! We were on an ocean. What could we do for food? I had to think. I had to be responsible for these friends. Aunt Rebekah would expect me to think of something. What could we do as a people?

Suddenly, I rose to the request. "I have Jack's fish-hooks," I said, astonished at myself.

Why hadn't I thought of that before? I was ashamed

that it took a woman's question to draw forth my answer. Like it or not, I was a leader.

Goshen clapped and laughed aloud. "Cassius," he called. They began a scheme to use belts and ropes for fishing line. Then Goshen took my shoulder.

"Below," he said. "I have had another matter in mind for some time. Ever since we took on cargo a couple of stops ago."

I led him down the ladder, and we stood aside as two came up to give us room. I recognized one as the man who led us in singing, but Goshen was talking again, pulling me around the walls in the dim, smelly hold. I slipped and fell in filth.

Men below were talking. "Chicken? I want me a pork chop with turnip greens."

"No pork chop for me. I want me some ham."

"High up on the hog, eh? You'd think the ocean would have fish?"

"It do. The captain and Mr. Kock had sea bass yesterday." Moans. Some laughter, nervous laughter.

Herein I must needs pause to tell you that Captain Lane was true to his oath. He swore he wouldn't stand around and watch us starve, and he didn't. He shouted orders from his bunkroom. Whenever he had to come on deck, he covered his nose with his elbow and stared straight out to sea.

Now below, Goshen patted the wall. "What's there?" he asked.

"A panel."

"Panel or door?"

"Panel. There's no knob or lock."

"Moz, open the panel. I smell food, root food."

How could he smell anything in that stench? Orders, always orders. I heard a shout on deck. Singing. What was going on? And how could I see to open a wall panel?

It was loose. I shook it and lifted it and twisted it until anger gave me strength to push it open. I crawled over the rim and found bags of white potatoes. With a penknife from Goshen's pouch, we cut chunks of raw potatoes to pass to people in the hold. I suppose this was stealing. Notwithstanding, there was a need to stay alive, and Aunt Rebekah would have approved.

If anyone told on us, I would be in trouble again. The very thought made my side pain, and reminded me of losing my garments.

Someone by the ladder called: "They've caught five fish up there." Goshen chuckled.

A woman said, "What good are five fish among so many?"

I laughed; the sound seemed strange from my throat. Would a miracle happen? We were feeding ourselves, not waiting for a white man to buy food for us. My side throbbed, but I thought now that I might live.

At that moment I began to wonder. What were my talents? How best could I serve people when I was grown?

From then on, we had food—food and work—which was just as important. Below deck, people kept the potato chunks passing. Day and night a working people fished for their own keep. From pants and pockets, belt hooks and needles and wire appeared for fishing. People lowered shirts and bloomers to scoop bits of plants and animals from the ocean surface to eat. As a people we had hope again. Perchance that was a miracle after all.

Mr. Kock was delighted. "How did you begin this fishing?" he asked. "Now you'll be strong for cotton farming."

"The boy Moses is our leader," they shouted.

Ha, I thought, maybe they had made a true appraisal. Eight hundred dollars I was worth. A generous sum. By the rail I confided in Goshen.

"You know Father Fitzpatrick thought he could sell me for eight hundred dollars?" With food in my stomach, I felt bolder. I leaned against the rail and watched a woman fishing. She had made a drag net from her bloomers, and with it she caught two funny flat little fish.

Goshen didn't answer me directly. He frowned and his lips were pressed tightly together as if he had just tasted vinegar. "Tell me about the clouds in the sky," he asked.

"Oh, they're beautiful. Puffy white in deep blue."

"Cumulus." He had been teaching me the names of cloud formations. A man by the name of Luke Howard had titled them in 1803. Knowing clouds proved how highly educated Goshen was.

"How much money do you think they're worth?"

"Goshen, that's foolish. Clouds aren't worth money."

"What color is the Atlantic?"

"Oh, right now there's a band of green here, then deep blue to the horizon." Someone shouted as he hauled a big fish aboard. Goshen and I were given raw clear chunks to eat. Chewy and wet, the fish was more delectable than lamb with mint or ham with applesauce to my hungry innards.

"And," Goshen said, "how much money do you think the ocean is worth?"

"Goshen, what are you trying to tell me?"

He held a hand to his chest. "I'm blind. How much money do you think I'm worth?"

"Oh, Goshen. You're a person. A most outstanding person."

"How much?"

Jokingly I said, "I wouldn't sell you." However, I was thinking that in his condition he wouldn't sell for much, and I was ashamed. I had grown to love him. Everyone felt so sorry that the blow on his head had blinded him. He no longer clung to me alone because everyone was friendly toward him.

One woman said, "He done adjusted to blindness so good."

"Goshen move like a man born blind," a man said.

In truth I learned that Goshen had only been blind about two years. Before adult measles and an eye infection following it, he had read and written, worked on land and sea. He was raised on Maryland's tobacco plantations, and educated beside a young master by tutors.

The captain ofttimes inquired about his vision. He really thought his sailor had caused the blindness. And Mr. Kock asked, "Is your vision returned yet, Goshen? It may, you know."

I think Mr. Kock and the captain felt a little guilty, and that was good. On plantations old people or people injured and blinded were put out into the woods to starve. If Mr. Kock felt guilty, perchance it meant that Goshen was safe.

At this time Goshen said, "I was sold three times. Should I judge my worth by what some master bought me for? Who can put a price on me?"

I was beginning to get the sum of his reasoning and I didn't want to hear any more of it. "Here's Sarah," I told Goshen. That would distract him!

Throughout the voyage Goshen persisted in asking me, "Tell me what that maiden looks like, Moz. Is she pretty?"

Ofttimes I grew weary of describing women for him. I discovered that through luffing sails, creaking boards and masts, sloshing water, whistling wind, popping jibs—he could hear a woman sigh. And he'd ask me what she looked like!

He talked to all the women, knew them by voice and name, and grieved as some of them died on the voyage.

Forthwith Sarah worked her way toward us with two men in tow. "They been having high fever and sores in they mouths," she said.

One man had a couple of sores on his face and on the inside of his elbow as well. The sores were separate red spots. Inside the mouth they were raised in bumps with fluid inside the bump like a volcano's lake in a mountain.

I described the sores to Goshen. "Smallpox," he said.

I knew that smallpox spread from person to person and killed many. My hands trembled. Around us people grew silent. They looked as if they would have moved away if there had been space.

8

Although each day seemed an eternity, from Annapolis sailing down our Eastern Coast took only about two weeks in my summation. For another week or so after we passed Florida, from sailors' comments, I knew we sailed along the Bahama Bank and around Cuba. Sailing through the Windward Passage we passed Tortuga Island, an island that belonged to Hayti and had been haven to pirates of old.

Finally one morning we sighted the mountainous island of Hayti itself. I calculated that we had arrived in the third week of January 1864.

Birds flew as thick as peas in a soup, and their cries were glorious to the ear. We arrived at a bay with embracing arms of green land and guarded by the large island of Gonâve. Below us I could gaze through clear water and see ridges of colorful pink and tan coral.

Now I suffered from heat as much as I had suffered from cold when we set off. From standing or hunger or both, my legs and feet were swollen and stiff. I had to carry Jack's coat since there was nowhere to lay anything down. With

Goshen's penknife, I cut slits in my shoe tops to relieve my swollen feet. Other, older people had legs more swollen than mine were.

The captain ordered sailors to lower anchor, and Mr. Kock called, "Gentlemen, we're at the Republic of Hayti!"

Notwithstanding the heat, he dressed nattily in suit coat and derby like a red-comb rooster. "I'll go talk to the officials about our colony," he said.

The captain ordered a rowboat to take him to the city. The ship had avoided shallow reefs of coral by anchoring far from shore. The city shimmered in heat waves like a friendly face in fog. It sprouted many square stone buildings of commerce, and a cathedral-looking building or two with spires. Low-lying homes in squares of pink and blue and yellow zigzagged up the mountainside.

Watching Mr. Kock leave gave me much pleasure. It was good to have arrived. For a week and a half I had fed on fish and seaweed and potatoes and I felt stronger. When the captain discovered that his supply of potatoes was gone, he argued with Mr. Kock, not us.

"I hold you blighty right to blame!" yelled the captain. "Them poor black wretches were starving."

"I'll have credit on Hayti," said Mr. Kock. "They'll refill the supply for your return trip. Don't be anxious, Captain Lane." Mr. Kock had stroked the captain's shirtsleeve, but the captain jerked away from him. Now we had arrived at Hayti.

We watched the rowboat ride the waves to shore at Port-au-Prince. Later I learned that this western third of Hispaniola Island had been the Republic of Hayti since

1804. Above the city, mountain sides were green and tan in small patches of farms.

The top slopes seemed covered with a thin pine forest. I saw narrow streams winding downhill winking, blinking, and playing peekaboo with sunlight. Lower down, leafy trees took the place of the pine.

"Tell me what you see, Moz," Goshen said shaking my arm. Thank heaven no one else called me Moz. I was Moses!

"We're miles from shore," I told him. I described the close shoreline. "Low trees with dark green leaves are wading out into the water like shorebirds."

"Sounds like mangrove trees."

"And those birds calling like crows are green and yellow."

"Maybe parrots." He sighed and smiled.

"The air is fragrant."

"Tropical flowers in bloom," he said.

People whispered. Excitement rippled over us in the heat like a breeze over still waters. We were a people interwoven with hopeful expectancy. Thus I saw smiles all around me.

"Now we'll eat twice a day," Cassius said from the rail.

"Maybe three times," someone else said, laughing.

"Our farmland is on the other side."

"Cotton ready for chopping and rice lands are planted in the gullies. Now we a free people for real," a woman said.

Sarah moaned. "How we gonna get home from this Cow Island? I wanna go back to Virginia." No one answered her.

On the tranquil water tiny white puffs drifted like cumulus clouds on a tiny world. I pointed and looked to a sailor leaning on the rail beside me.

"Sea smoke," the sailor said. Usually the sailors ignored us. Except to shove us aside, they seldom spoke.

"Sea smoke?" I asked softly. "What makes it happen?"

He glanced around before answering. "When the water is warmer than the air, you get sea smoke." He shoved himself away from the rail as if embarrassed to be seen talking to me.

My heart leaped from my throat for jubilation. I fell in love with Hayti. The sky was magnificent, the land stretched high with majestic mountains, and sparkling blue rivers flowed. Goshen and I kept moving, allowing people from the center to stand by the rails, allowing people below to come above deck.

The long journey and fishing together night and day had made the people into teams like families. People looked out for one another, took responsibility for one another.

Unfortunately, by then ten or fifteen men and two women were ill with fever and pox sores. Since they could not stand, they lay on the deck. We fed them and gave them extra shares of our water allotments.

For hours Mr. Kock did not return.

Soon the very air seemed to be restless. Off the starboard I saw a waterspout, then three more. The whirling water threw silver spray high in the air for several minutes. I smelled the salt of the sea. How I yearned to swim in the clear cool waters.

Back at St. Mary's Aunt Rebekah would sit on shore

sewing, and I would swim in the Potomac. That was on summer Sundays while Father Fitzpatrick said Mass, and we had a couple of hours free. Those were gladsome times. Now Rebekah was dead, and I was in summer weather in the month of January!

In truth this was like a dream. A nightmare some would say. Enticed aboard a ship for work—hungry, seasick, lonely—for a voyage of some three weeks; disease and death walking amongst us; and now we faced what was Mr. Kock's great colony dream.

I was no farmer or field hand—what role would I play in this colony? How could I use my house-slave talents? Would people still need me?

While we waited for Mr. Kock's return, a man named Jacob began to sing. His voice I had heard before. Notwithstanding the odors below, he always sang softly down there. At first it was lullabys. Then his wife and infant died, and he sang hymns. One of his favorites began, "Nobody knows the trouble I seen, nobody knows but Jesus."

Now as he stood near us on deck, he sang a rousing song called "Old Abe Has Gone and Did It, Boys!" It went like this:

Gather round ye darkies all
Listen to my singing
Draw de bow and play de bones
Set de banjo ringing
Old 'mancipation coming
Dis here darky hear dem say
In de house dis morning

Dat de Yankee so-jer boys
And old Abe was coming
Old 'mancipation coming. . . .

He stood near me, so I asked, "Did you make that song up? It behooves me to tell you I like it."

He smiled and tried to step back from me. "Moses," he said, "a friend of mine done wrote this one. He be S. Fillmore Bennett, and in Chicago in 1862 they done printed up his song."

I had never thought of publishing songs, but someone sure had printed the hymn music for St. Mary's. "I'm most grateful for your singing, Jacob," I said. He bowed.

Known to all, I was highly respected among the people. Sarah and Cassius thought I was smart like Goshen, and ofttimes I let them think it. When I described ocean fish or cloud formations, I gave them names from Goshen, but I gave the names as if they were my own. Oh, deceit, your name is Moses!

In the afternoon when we saw the sailors bringing Mr. Kock back, we were all in high spirits. However, a boat of black men in short-sleeve gray uniforms seemed to be chasing the rowboat. One of them shouted in French, "C'est imposteur!"

"It's an imposter," or "it's fraud," or "he's a hypocrite," was what that meant. He rattled off many other words with frequent "non," meaning "no," and "ne'st," meaning "is not." All of it sounded most discouraging.

People shoved and pushed around me asking what this

meant. I translated the French words as I caught on to them, and Goshen passed them on.

When they reached our ship, the man spoke to Captain Lane in English. "What lease? He had no lease for Isle à Vache. Why did you bring this imposter here?"

"These blacks are from the States," said Captain Lane, pointing to us. "Mr. Kock here wants a colony. There's hundreds of black people like you for that island, and I'm not about to be taking them back." He practically spit out the words.

A sighing breeze was the only sound on deck. Masts groaned and sails luffed impatiently in that breeze. The men from Hayti conferred with one another. They argued in French, but much too rapidly for me to understand. Finally the man who had spoken before said, "Leave them. We will write your government in protest. Let them try farming there until boats come for them." He saluted our captain and rowed away in his boat.

Elbow across nose, Captain Lane went below to his quarters.

Mr. Kock climbed aboard, still smiling. He made his way through the crowd onto the raised quarterdeck.

Hands clasped behind him, sweat running down his face, he said, "Men, I will establish a colony on Cow Island that will make President Abraham Lincoln jealous! And you"—his voice actually broke in midsentence—"you wonderful colored people will do it for me."

Everyone was silent. I wondered if he thought we were deaf. We had heard everything. Didn't he realize that?

"Let's hear a cheer," he called. "Hip, hip . . ." We all stared at him. My skin began to crawl as if ants were on me.

"We can sing," he said. "Where's our singer? My country 'tis of thee, sweet land of liberty. . . ."

His tenor voice was pleasant, but that was the wrong song to sing. Sarah began loud weeping. Tears of homesickness slid down my cheeks like rain on a riverbank. Both men and women sobbed.

Mr. Kock gave his own little cheer, "Hip, hip, hooray!" and went below. Rather British notwithstanding a German accent, I thought.

The sailors pulled anchor. We scraped a coral reef—that brought an angry captain up—and we began to sail for Cow Island. I estimated the distance carefully. It was around an embrace of land and on the southwest side of Hayti. Soon we we would see our new home.

 **9**

As a further omen of ill, as we sailed toward Cow Island one of the men with smallpox was suddenly taken from us by the hand of death. This time we washed and dressed him ourselves. Jacob sang "Nobody Knows the Trouble I Seen." I led the Lord's Prayer and added a Hail Mary. Then I recited the Prologue to St. John's Gospel, which Father Fitzpatrick had made me memorize.

Although it didn't pertain to death, I recited it slowly and solemnly. Notwithstanding the occasion, it touched my soul at the deepest, and seemed to touch the others as well.

When I finished, everyone was silent for a long time. Goshen said, "The Lord giveth and the Lord taketh away. Blessed be the name of the Lord!"

Everyone shouted, "Amen!"

Men by the rail released the man's body to the deep. In Latin I whispered, "May perpetual light shine upon him, and may he rest in peace."

I hadn't even known his name. Later I regretted that I never learned names and made accurate counts of the people living and dying on the boat and on Cow Island. Neither the captain nor Mr. Kock had real numbers, either.

Colored people didn't matter to them, but they should have mattered to me.

At this point we colored people had buried our own at sea for the first time. I throbbed with a good feeling. We were taking charge of our own lives and our own deaths. How I admired those people. Excepting me and Goshen, they were uneducated, but most smart, and gloriously capable of suffering, forgiving, and loving. Brave. Courageous.

I felt ashamed of my arrogance.

But I wanted my own clothes. Didn't I have a right to them? Mr. Kock didn't own me. We were about to leave ship. Could I approach Jack? My face grew warm every time I saw him in my fine white shirt. Jack with corn silk yellow hair and bleached gray eyes. Jack wearing my clothes from St. Mary of the Sea!

I wove a path toward him, but felt resentment of his whiteness grow as I drew nearer. At that moment I hated the whiteness that called me slave, and the blackness that revealed the curse of that slavery on me. The uncomplaining man's death and burial that morning had stirred my deepest emotions. I was truly bereft.

And I was embarrassed. To think that I had measured my worth in money. A blind man had taught me to see. And I had even thought of Goshen's worth in a sale of money. What a slave mentality I had. My face grew warm in shame.

I felt my hands ball into fists. My swollen feet ached. As I limped around people toward Jack, I struggled to separate him from his whiteness. The good Father had blue eyes and white skin. I was angry at the good Father. Mr. Kock had white skin. I was angry at him. He was greedy and abused us, forced us into starvation. In my mind I tried to reason that white people were human, but reason didn't penetrate my deepest emotional self.

Jack saw me coming. I folded his jacket. A smile glimmered on his thin rosy lips. His nose was as sharp as an ax. He edged toward me, and we met at the mainmast. I had taken off his shirt.

"You wanting your clothes back, Moses?" he asked. "I'm most sorry about Mr. Kock doing that. You looking forward to your island? I'd give a fine penny to live on an island."

I shrugged. Here we were, two boys, and I was repulsed by his color, or lack of it. We could have been friends. What was wrong with me?

What could I say? My throat felt choked like a chimney with a stork's nest. I held his jacket out and took Goshen's coin purse into my hand. Jack began undressing too.

He chattered on. "Once I knew me some sailors who were marooned on an island. They fished and swam. Sounded most enjoyable to me. You thinking hard on it?"

Again I shrugged. I put on my shirt. My pants were all right, but my underclothes smelled like Jack. Men turned their backs and stood around us as we dressed again. I had stripped without thinking of the women.

"If I get to row, I'll set foot on your island. I row strong as any man."

Jack sounded young, younger than I. Rebekah always said I was too old. She told me I never had a childhood, a

chance to run and play with children my age. By five or six I
was house slave to an old priest. She told me I was too serious. In truth, I didn't find things funny. How could I? I spent
my life pleasing the good Father, and he was most hard to
please.

Before me Jack's eyes were really pale, gray with yellow
flecks. I asked him, "Would you tell me how old you are?"

He grinned. A nice grin. He was missing several teeth,
knocked out I suppose. "Go on now," he said. "You tell me,
then I'll tell you."

He was playful like a kitten with yarn. I often wound
yarn for Aunt Rebekah. She'd had a yellow kitten, soft and
furry with a raspy little tongue. But it had died.

I sighed. Some of my revulsion was easing. Jack was
human in spite of his bleached body. Perchance I could be
playful too.

Bending over, I could hardly get my feet into my pants.
I dared not remove my shoes because I could never get them
back on. While I struggled, Jack supported me. His touch
unnerved me.

"Guess my age," I said. "If you are within a measure or
two, I'll give you a prize." In an instant I knew what I would
give him. The only possession I had.

"You first," he said, "and me, I'll give you a fine prize."

What could he give me? I was curious. Father Fitzpatrick said worldly curiosity was all vanity. But I stayed
curious, and that meant another chain broken.

"You're seventeen," I said.

He laughed. "Aye, tall for my age, but younger."

"I'm fourteen."

"Fourteen? I'm fifteen. Moses, we both about the same."

I stared at him. Knowing we were the same age melted the last of my feelings of repugnance.

Softly he asked, "You ever know your ma or pa?"

I shook my head no.

"Neither me."

I fumbled in the coin purse. "Here," I said, "take your prize." I pulled out the brass button.

His eyes danced, and he grinned. He seemed delighted.

"Wait," he said. Already dressed, he slipped away and back before I closed my pants. "Here you be."

He gave me a long pearl-handle knife in a thick leather scabbard. It was perfect for peeling potatoes or shelling clams or scaling fish. It would slip on my good leather belt, which he had returned. His pants had been been held up by a piece of rope.

"I'm most grateful," I said.

"I like this," said Jack. "I have a button collection."

"You do? I did once." In truth, a moment before, I had had one. We stared at each other. Same size, about the same age, same collection.

I heard Goshen coming. "Moses," he called, "describe the clouds at starboard."

Catching his hand, I ducked under the mast and looked. In seconds the clouds drew nearer.

"A straight layer of dark cirrus, cirrostratus, moving fast," I told him. The thick pile of black clouds with feathery edges looked like a heaping of black crow feathers from a dead bird. Or maybe it was like a thick black wool blanket with raveled selvage. High winds struck us that instant out of nowhere.

Sailors didn't wait for orders. The crew shouted to the captain, and Jack was up in the rigging in a second.

"No wonder we saw water spouts this morning," a sailor called. "Bad omen. All of this." He pointed to us.

"Not the season for hurricanes," another called.

"Down here there can be hurricanes at any season," another man shouted. By then the wind was louder than the roar of a train engine.

Forthwith, someone called, "Isle à Vache portside."

I bent over and dragged Goshen with me to the rail on the other side of our clipper.

Notwithstanding the storm's threat, I wanted to see our island. Cow Island, at long last.

10

The ship began to skip and bounce on high waves. Wood creaked and waves sloshed over the deck. I heard a moan as the crew secured all doors. The people below deck were trapped, shut off from us. To steady him, I put Goshen's hand on the rail, and I stared at Isle à Vache.

Sailing now across the wind and rain, and around the edge of the island, I saw how narrow it was. Later I learned it was two miles wide and eight miles long. A number of miles, perhaps five or six, separated it from the southern shore of the bigger island of Hispaniola, where Hayti was.

On the way we had passed two other islands. Gonâve guarded the bay, and Tortuga we saw at a distance. Tortuga meant "turtle" in Spanish. Were the Turtle and Cow Islands shaped like a turtle and a cow? Were there turtles on Turtle Island and cows on Cow Island?

Notwithstanding the darkening skies, Cow Island looked pretty. At the edge some places it was sandy and like a desert. On other areas it was rocky with a thick pine forest rising up a hill. Mangrove trees were on other shores.

Our clipper scraped a reef, and tottered on this coral hill. Goshen and I clung to the railing. Just as I thought the boat would dip into the sea, wind caught in a sail and our clipper slid off the reef.

"Sail south-southwest!" shouted Captain Lane. The wind was screaming down the ocean waves. We were rain soaked and I could barely catch my breath. Someone among us caught my elbow. Yes!

We crouched arm in arm holding one another down. The rain washing over the deck covered my face and took my breath, but it was warm and cleansing to my skin, my clothes. Sailors walked on our backs crossing the deck because we were linked like pickets in a fence, arm in arm, and interwoven with knees hooked.

The clipper sailed to deeper water. Sailors lowered anchor and reefed the sails, struggling against the wind. Part of me was afraid and lonely while another part enjoyed the power of the storm: the roaring wind, the sheets of rain. When the clipper rose on a swell of ocean, I could see the mountains of Hispaniola. When the ship slid down into a water trough, we were so low I only saw waves standing around us as high as the masts.

"What's it like?" Goshen called.

I could hardly hear him in the roar of wind and water, and he was shouting in my ear.

"Black clouds streaking in the wind."

"Nimbostratus," he said, and asked, "any funnel clouds, or dipping blackness?"

While people held my feet, I stood on tiptoe to look all around. "No dipping darkness," I said, "in fact the sky is light to the west-southwest."

As rapidly as the storm struck, a calm descended.

"Goshen," I said, "I can see the storm whipping up the sea far over there."

Now the air was rich with sea smells. Sailors loosened the main halyard and brought the mainsail to three-quarters.

Because we had held one another, no one had been washed overboard. When the crew opened the hatches, Goshen and I took a turn below deck. Coming from fresh salt air with rich aromas of sea plants and fish, I found the smell below even more unbearable.

I felt so clean and fresh, I tried not to touch against the walls or fall onto the floor. We stood near the potato storage place. All the potatoes were gone. My innards had learned to manage on one sea biscuit, two cups of water, and what fish I caught, eaten raw, and what sea plants I hooked.

When we were back on deck, Cow Island looked rather tattered from the storm. Branches and limbs of trees floated in the water. The rocky coast was littered with silvery fish and huge strands of brown and red and green sea plants. Already huge birds were cleaning up the shore.

Captain Lane called Mr. Kock up. "Are you blighty right ready to go ashore with your colony, mister?"

"Ah, Captain, thank you greatly for the safe pleasant voyage. Yes, indeed, tomorrow morning we can choose somewhere to go ashore."

"This evening, you"—Captain Lane turned and pointed to us—"and those stinking people will go ashore. Prepare your trunks and chest."

"Captain," Mr. Kock said, smiling, "I have to select our landing site."

"The island. Now."

"But, sir, it's a jungle right there. Farther around there's a sandy beach. And surely you'll use a gangplank to shore?"

"Prepare the boats," Captain Lane ordered. "These here people are going ashore now!"

"Ah, Captain, you mean to explore?"

"Now." Arms folded, the captain worked his way over to the side to watch the lowering of three boats. "Mr. Kock, we ain't going no closer," he called. "This here island is ringed with coral reefs. Our boats are readying."

Mr. Kock's smile faded. The sun was low, and so were our spirits. I felt a tug on my shirt. Jack pulled me over to the mizzenmast. Hand on my shoulder, Goshen followed.

"Good thing you're leaving in the dark, Moses," said Jack. "Our fellows wanna sneak a barrel of water to shore for you. They saying some of these smaller islands have no fresh water. And we're doubting they'll supply you from Hayti. Seeing as though they don't approve of Mr. Kock and all."

I nodded. "Water."

"Open the barrel to refill in the rain, and collect all the fresh water you can," Jack said.

One barrel of water? I sure hoped there was water on land. For our hundreds of people, a barrel would last a short time at most. Anyway, how often did it rain?

A sailor said to Jack, "Tell 'bout the birds."

"Watch what birds eat," Jack said. "Them leaves and berries that pigeons and parrots and guinea hens eat probably ain't poisonous. What the snakes and lizards eat might likely be."

I felt as if the sky had lowered onto my shoulders. More

problems? Surely now we would have some small comforts like beds and meals?

Goshen asked, "Aren't there people to greet us? Bunkhouses for workers?"

I couldn't answer. To Jack I nodded. "I'm grateful."

"And they do have crocodiles," he added. "Besides sharks. So be careful where you swim. Too close to land and there's crocs, too far out there's sharks. I know what I'm talking 'bout."

"I'm most grateful, Jack."

He touched my arm and ran to obey an order.

Mr. Kock had a sailor haul his trunks and sea chests on deck. Meanwhile, about twenty to twenty-five to a boat, three boats at a time, people were rowed across water as shiny as a mirror and golden in sunset rays.

Our sunset that evening was glorious. Fluffy cumulus clouds bounced hues of red and rose and lavender restlessly among themselves like bustling ladies dressed for a benefit ball. Four rainbows arched over the Caribbean Sea caressing the waves in teasing colors, colors reversed from one rainbow to the other. And the burning sun was a tender golden yellow as it seemed to sink into the waters without even hissing.

Goshen and I hung back. Sarah, Cassius, and Simeon stood by us. "Are there people there to get us settled? Tell me what you see, Moz," Goshen asked.

"Nothing. Rien. Nada. Goshen, we're going to an island with nobody but Mr. Kock with his sea chests."

Cassius said, "I done thought there would be boss men and cabins for us."

"Maybe you just can't see them," said Goshen. He couldn't tell that Mr. Kock was nearby.

"Men," said Mr. Kock, who had overheard, "we are going to build our own shelters, farm the land in cotton, and sell our crop this fall." He was smiling again.

As soon as Mr. Kock passed, Cassius said, "We in big trouble now."

"Out of the frying pan and into the fire," Simeon said.

Sarah said, "I wanna go home to Virginia. How am I gonna get back to Virginia?" No one answered her.

As the last colored to leave the ship, we carried those ill with smallpox—five men delirious with fever. In the rowboat I wet their arms and burning foreheads with salty seawater. Aunt Rebekah used to cool feverish people with water. More than a dozen others among us seemed better from the pox.

When our rowboat scraped on rocks, I jumped out and waded. There were ten of us and five sick. I carried a man, William, by his head and shoulders, trying not to fall on rocks slippery with green growth. Goshen carried William by his legs. We were on Cow Island at last.

11

On an island, when the sun sinks into the western sea, darkness covers you suddenly like a cloak pulled over the face. Following others, Goshen and I pushed in darkness through mangrove roots to climb onto solid land. There we must needs lay this William down, as we were exhausted. Forthwith we heard the surrounding land sounds: frogs peeping, birds murmuring, sleepy insects singing in harmony, mosquitoes whining.

Land felt strange to the legs. Flat seemed odd as I placed each foot down. Used to the ship's constant movements, I now felt most unsteady. In my head I was still swaying with the clipper.

"Over here," Jacob called, and waved for us to follow him.

Goshen swung William over his shoulder, and I guided Goshen. For half an hour our last boatload of people pushed through woodland hung with vines until we reached at long last a sandy clearing. Men had pulled storm-broken branches aside. Our friends were spread out there, lying down in comfort for the first time in weeks.

Sarah called us to lay William down beside the others

who were ill with smallpox. Skirts pulled around her, she sat with her knees drawn up and her head resting on them. I couldn't understand Sarah sitting like that until I touched the back of her neck. She was hot—burning with fever.

"I'll get you water," I said. "Goshen, Sarah's ill."

"The water barrel, did they leave it for us?" Goshen asked.

I found Mr. Kock staring at the sand and surrounded by three trunks and our water barrel. That night I carried water for Sarah and the others who were sick. The rest of them stood in lines, dipping and drinking from two ladles and Goshen's cup. Fresh water served as our supper.

That first night on Cow Island was heavenly. How marvelous to lie down on clean, fresh-smelling sand. Aches from everywhere on myself appeared, and disappeared. I lay staring at a million sparkling stars. Their worth, like mine, was immeasurable.

All the beauty and goodness on earth were free for persons to rejoice in. For all the people on earth. How dare some people keep others as slaves? What injustice! How dare they buy, own, sell other human beings?

Now I must needs understand more of what Aunt Rebekah had told me. I felt so free. Thrilled with permission to be myself. I owned my soul, always had the right to, and no one or nothing would cheat me out of it, I vowed!

Shortly after sunrise, we were sun-scalded in humidity and heat. As screeching birds dived for dead fish, the sun hammered us under its light. Mr. Kock called us all together.

"Men," he said smiling, "here are tools and cotton-seeds. You may now lay out your farms for growing cotton."

I saw seven hoes, three rakes, and a dozen or so shovels. There were bundles of seed. A dozen shovels for all those men and women?

The hand of death had reduced our numbers. Besides all five or seven infants, about thirty or forty adults had gone to glory. Called to heaven, and I never knew their names. Yet we were still a group of some size.

Someone asked Mr. Kock, "Where do we 'spected to farm, boss, the woods or the stones or the sand?"

Mr. Kock raised an arm. "Now, men, at long last, I am Governor Kock of Isle à Vache. We are a colony." His smile seemed plastered on his face.

Hot breezes blew tattered clothing, but we were no longer a confused crowd of strangers. People asked:

"Where's our cabins, boss man?"

"Where's our food, boss man?"

"Boss, how all us gonna farm with them few tools?"

"Please," called Governor Kock, "I am Governor to you now. Not boss or boss man." I thought of that gilded sign in his bunkroom. That title must have been most important to him. "I'll entertain more questions," he said.

Or course he hadn't answered any of the other questions. And he didn't answer now, except to wave to us and ask for further questions. At first I thought he would answer them all together, but he refrained from doing so. My spirit grew faint within me, and I suspected others felt the same.

For a while, no one spoke. Notwithstanding, this German stood smiling, with thumbs hooked in his belt.

Goshen spoke: "Boss—"

"Call me Governor, please. I am governor of Isle à Vache at long last."

"Boss," repeated Goshen, ignoring his order, "how long do you think that barrel of water will last all these people?"

Mr. Kock's face grew rosy. Goshen had deliberately disobeyed his order. That was insubordination, insolence, impudence, being uppity, acting obstinate. I felt like cheering. Another chain fell from my shoulders.

Everyone watched Mr. Kock. I think for the first time he realized that he was the only white man on a tiny island with hundreds of colored people. Looking around, he pointed to Goshen and chuckled.

"Goshen, I put you in charge of water. Find our rivers and streams." He waved. "All of you, get busy working. Stake out your farms."

With those words, he put hands behind his back, turned, and stood. There was nowhere for him to go; no quarterdeck, no bunkroom, no captain's quarters. He and his trunks were out in glaring white sunlight on a glaring white-sand beach.

He plowed forward, walking through sand, and touched one trunk. Looking over his shoulder, he opened and closed his mouth. I think he was about to ask someone to move it for him, and he thought better of it. He began to drag the leather trunk toward shade. Someone took pity on him. "Boss man, where you want we should move your trunks?"

In a low voice Goshen said, "Moses, wave the people over to a meeting in the shade, if possible." Shade wasn't possible for all those people. We met in a curved island theater of sculptured sand with the stage for me and Goshen at the seashore. From tree line to sea, people sat, crouched, stood.

Back to the sea and arms outstretched, Goshen stood. "Brothers and sisters," he said, "look around. We're on this island for better or worse. You know we're folks who know how to work. You know we're a good people. Folks are needed to build shelters and latrines, to find food, to farm land."

"Is a supply ship coming?" someone called out.

Like the odor of sour milk a chuckle puffed among us.

Rusty Rich said, "I think we should wait and see." They called him Rusty Rich because his hair, skin, and eyes were reddish brown.

"And see what?" Goshen asked. "Let's set to work. Moz and me, we'll explore for water. Who will fish for food?"

A group volunteered, and others gave them fishhooks. "Be careful. Look out for sharks and crocodiles," I said. They walked off, about seventy people in one direction and fifty in the other.

"Us gonna build shelters from storms and rain and some latrines," someone offered. He went off with his group, taking a couple of shovels. Men ran to catch up. After three weeks on the boat, people seemed eager to start working.

"We'll go a-looking for land to grow cotton," one called over his shoulder. About a hundred straggled after him. With the rest of the shovels, hoes, and rakes over a few shoulders, they plowed through the fine sand in another direction. Those who were too weak lay down.

Goshen and I reached the shade of trees. "I don't care about my shoes," I said. "I just can't wear them anymore." I sat beside Goshen, who stared into space. After I pulled my shoes off, I hid them in a tree niche birds had used for a nest.

"Moz, how big you reckon this island is?" asked Goshen.

"It's narrow across, and I could see all of the length of it out there during the storm," I said. "Not too long, and high in the middle with peaks."

"And where is Hayti from here?" He rested chin on knees.

"We should be able to see it from the other side."

"They said they would write our government, Moz. Think they will?"

I shrugged, but of course Goshen couldn't see it. "What will they say?" I asked. "That Mr. Kock has no lease for Isle à Vache?" I leaned against the tree trunk.

"Moz, they must also know that we can't farm here. Malaria, smallpox, we'll all die." He sighed.

"Goshen," I said, "you never sounded like this before." I was astonished at his pessimism. Myself, I was filled with hope.

"We'll try, of course," he said, "but I want you to know that you will have to swim over to Hayti and get us rescued from this Cow Island."

"Me?"

"You. Let's explore now. Tell me what you see." He stood.

I was so astonished, I could hardly rise. My tender feet were still puffy, and striped from where the shoes had bound them. "Goshen, are you sure we can't do it?"

"I'm sure. Don't say anything until the others are sure

as well. It won't be long. Then you'll have to make a journey."

I put his hand on my shoulder.

Goshen was seldom wrong. I slapped at mosquitoes. Where mosquitoes lived, people sometimes suffered malaria. My mother had died of it. I remembered when a priest who visited Father Fitzpatrick suffered a recurrence of malaria. It had been in midsummer, but he shook so with a chill that his brass bed chattered on the floor at St. Mary's.

As we walked past, men and women moved Sarah and other feverish people to shade in the woods. Several women and a man gave the sick water. Men began breaking off branches and pulling up brush to clear ground space, and that space became the hospital. I sure hoped Sarah lived to see Virginia again.

And how would I reach Hayti across those miles of water? Surely Goshen was wrong.

12

On board the clipper I had lost count of days, but here on the island I planned to put a pebble in my left shoe for each one. And I decided that this first day was Sunday, whether or not that was true.

Before Goshen and I left to explore, I put in the first pebble. We walked along a ridge. "What do you see, Moz?"

"It's rocks and little pebbles up a slope. These pine trees are dwarfs compared to Maryland pines."

"No farmland? No water?"

"Birds like unto chickens are pecking at leaves over there."

"Let's gather some leaves," he said. "And, Moz, you have to sneak extra food and water for yourself. You and me, we're the healthiest people on this island. Remember you'll have to swim for Hayti." He squeezed my arm, patted my back. "Verily, prepare yourself, Moz."

Moses! That "Moz" whined in my ear like a mosquito I couldn't slap. I gathered some leaves, and we both ate. They tasted bitter and were prickly, but filling. We gathered some for his leather pouch and strolled on. Nearby a vine held yellow gourds. Old gourds were hollow with dry seeds that shook inside.

"Goshen, do you want your coin purse back?"

"Keep it. When we return, those gold coins will buy us a few weeks' lodging at some nice colored lady's boarding-house."

We walked along the mountain slope. "It's covered with prickly, waxy-leaf plants," I told him.

"Desert plants like out west."

"You're right, Goshen." I guided him around a boulder.

"Without fresh water, you can't farm a desert. What now?"

"There's a valley through the hills. Maybe we could cross the island and see Hayti." Slowly we made a path through the rocks. My tender feet were burning, cut by stones, and bleeding. Nevertheless I hopped along. I warned Goshen of snakes sunning themselves on rocks. I didn't know which ones were poisonous. The heat was intense among the boulders.

As we walked, I looked for water, but in truth I saw no stream or spring. We climbed up and down until I saw open sky ahead. "Goshen, we've arrived at the other shore."

"What do you see, Moz?"

"Hayti. There's a little city there. Rows of colorful houses creep up the hillside. But that's quite a ways over the water." I walked out into the water to cool my painful feet, but the salt stung every little cut.

"I don't suppose it's close enough to see any pretty maidens?" Goshen asked.

Hayti was miles away. The houses were pink and yellow dots on the gray hillside. Farm squares looked like green postage stamps, and perchance some antlike movement might be people.

"Hey, Goshen, there's one."

"Is she gladsome pretty, Moz?"

"I reckon she's the prettiest woman I ever did see."

"Tell me, Moz."

"Her brown skin shines like satin. Her eyes are sparkling like stars at night. Teeth are pearly white, and she's wearing an orange turban and sky-blue dress."

"Is it long?"

"What?"

"Her dress."

"It shows her slim ankles. Gladsome pretty, Goshen."

He sighed and sat on the shore to hug his knees. "You're a kind and descriptive liar, Moz. Nonetheless, thank you."

I laughed. "Goshen, were you ever married?"

"Yes, and no," he said. "I was never married by the Book. Three masters put me with women, but I wasn't allowed to stay by them. And I don't know where my children are kept."

He bent his face to the ground, and his eyes grew moist. My father was like that. Did he ever wonder about me?

I was staring across the sea to Hayti. The distance was one I would never be able to swim. I was a summer river-boy swimmer. And sharks? Crocodiles? I moaned.

"Wide?" asked Goshen.

"Most assuredly wide," I said. I thought, if this was our

only means of rescue, we were doomed. But I didn't tell Goshen.

That day we not only walked across Cow Island, but we walked along one whole length. Nowhere did we find fresh water.

That night back at our campsite, we ate those chicken-like birds roasted in campfires on the beach. Fish, cleaned and split into butterfly flaps, were hanging on spines to dry. While we were eating in groups on the beach, big birds dived for the drying fish. Men took turns waving shirts to scare off birds.

After dinner Goshen called another meeting. Our pattern became meetings every morning and evening. This time Goshen simply stood and let people talk.

"I walked all the way around the island," one man said. "There's precious little ground for planting."

"Mostly desert or mountain rocks, and the woods is wet salt land," his friend announced.

Goshen asked, "You gentlemen see any water? I didn't."

Funny, that blind Goshen always talked about "seeing." Even when he would say, "I see what you mean," I had to smile.

"No water."

"None that I see."

A woman said, "That water barrel be half empty now. In all this heat, a body needs to drink."

"We standing in the need of water all right."

Several people moaned. Others passed word about the barrel.

"Food, likewise," Rusty Rich said. "We done killed half

the guinea hens on this island for tonight's supper. We gonna starve."

Mr. Kock sat at a distance, but listened to all the reports. He ate sparsely. I wondered what he was feeling and thinking.

"We'll depend on fish," said a man. "Dry the fish the way my pappy showed me. Some of you getting over the pox can sit cleaning fish and shooing the birds off."

"These leaves are bitter, but birds eat them," I said. I walked around showing everybody our discovery.

"Good work, Moses!" Men and women patted my back.

"Of course," I said, "if we eat them all up, we won't have any." When I returned to Goshen's side, I realized what he had known from the start. This island could barely keep us alive; it couldn't provide a farming colony.

Three days later, we lay weakly in the shade. Our water had given out, and our only liquid was from leaves and raw wet fish. Mr. Kock looked worse than any of the rest of us. Red-faced, he had a fever that made him shiver and shake. He had muttered in German all night.

"Malaria," said Goshen.

I walked slowly on the beach that night. By moonlight I saw a wet spot in the sand. I was so thirsty, I threw myself down, dug frantically, and sipped the water. It wasn't too salty.

I trotted slowly back to our colony.

"Dig in the sand," I called in a husky voice. "The water

that comes up is less salty." My throat was so dry. I couldn't speak louder. I walked from group to group telling them.

I dragged Goshen to drink from my pool. Even the gritty sand tasted good.

After that we had pools we sipped from day and night. During the day we covered them to keep them from evaporating.

The humidity and heat drained away our strength, but still we worked. The little land farmed lay dry and dusty. We only had cottonseeds, no seeds for food crops; and without fresh water, no cottonseeds sprouted.

Over half the people worked at spearing fish with sharpened sticks or at tending the sick. As soon as fish were brought in, others scaled and cleaned them. Still others cut them for drying in the sun. While working, people sang, joked, and told tall tales. Leaders sprang up in several groups, and they all referred to Goshen or me to decide arguments.

I found myself deciding such things as requiring that people take turns calling when to stop for the day; and determining that women would always eat first; and ordering that we avoid killing guinea hens because they were so few now.

At one meeting Jacob said, "We need fish-drying sheds, like they used back home for tobacco." Some men built them. After that birds couldn't steal our fish through the sheds' slatted roofs.

The spearfishing I volunteered for was a gladsome task. At morn before sunrise I would stand in cool water up to my knees. I fished in my underwear. If I stood most still, fish would nibble at my legs. Jabbing with the spear was an art. I learned to jab a hair's breadth ahead of where the fish would dart.

More than once I jabbed my own foot.

Once a sleek gray shark streaked toward me, his fin cutting through the sea. My bleeding foot had attracted him. I splashed water getting away from that eye, those dagger-sharp teeth. But the shark followed till it was floundering in shallow water.

I sneaked extra fish and ate a few leaves three times a day. To grow stronger, I swam by the mangrove roots every evening.

Goshen said, "Moz, I hear raw meat gives strength."

After that, I ate my ocean fish raw. Besides, we were rapidly using up all the dry wood on the island. Green wood burned smoky to keep mosquitoes away, but wouldn't burn hot enough to cook fish. Those dry yellow gourds burned well.

The mosquitoes didn't give me that much grief. By day there was a hot breeze along the beach that kept them away. And I avoided the woodlands, where they swarmed.

Mr. Kock grew better of malaria, but something else had happened to him. Fully dressed, he would sit all day in shady water by mangrove roots and stare out to sea. Time after time he called me over.

"How's the cotton growing, Moses?"

"There isn't any cotton, sir."

"Is it high now? Are they chopping cotton?"

"There isn't any cotton, sir."

"That's good. Keep up your spirits, Moses. I'll show President Lincoln the best cotton-farming colony ever."

We had nursed him when he was ill, and now we fed him. A woman washed his clothes.

One day two more of us died: a woman with malaria following smallpox, and a man who had appeared to have recovered from smallpox. We buried them deep in the sand, side by side. Goshen and I carried stones to set as headstones.

The interesting thing was, as I recited St. John's Prologue, I saw water rising around their bodies in the graves.

The next day Goshen and I began digging wells. When they were finished, sand blew in, but we could climb down rocky steps and find six inches of only slightly salty water.

I continued to count the days with pebbles, and I told everyone what day of the week it was. That organized us.

We worked hard weekdays, but no one worked Saturday evening or Sunday. Robert the Preacher and Jacob the Singer held church services every Saturday night and all day Sunday.

After several weeks a new wave of smallpox struck, and one day I saw bumps in Goshen's mouth. Soon Goshen was lying low and likely to die. Would the hand of death take Goshen away from me the way it took Aunt Rebekah? I felt so low in spirits, I wept in the nights. But by day I led the meetings all by myself and tried to be cheerful.

13

Without Goshen to talk to, life became an intolerable burden. All of us missed him, because he had encouraged us all and had organized people at tasks; now that was my job. Because of the heat, I walked around only in underpants, as did most of the men. Women wore long skirts cut off at the knees. When I told Goshen that, he smiled in his fever.

Hour after hour I fed Goshen our Cow Island leaves and gave him sips of water. Twice a day I undressed him and washed him in seawater. Salt on his skin kept him ashy, but his pox sores seemed to heal quicker. After that everyone washed their sick ones two or three times a day with giant seashells of salt water.

Our days were filled with the same tasks over and over. People grew testy. A few stopped working, but came for food. Others remained cheerful and dutiful. Sarah recovered, but she was weak and weepy, especially when people sang. Jacob had another song I loved. These are the words as I remember them:

I'll be free, I'll be free, and none shall confine
With fetters and chains this free spirit.

From my youth have I vowed in my God to rely,
And despite the oppressor, gain freedom or die.

Tho' my back is all torn by the merciless rod,
Yet firm is my trust in the right arm of God.
In his strength I'll go forth and forever will be,
'Mong the hills of the North, where the bondsman is free.
'Mong the hills of the North, where the bondsman is free.

Let me go! Let me go! To the land of the brave,
Where shackles must fall from the limbs of the slave,
Where freedom's proud eagle screams wild thru' the sky,
And the sweet mountain birds in glad notes reply.

Jacob said it was written in 1845 by a man named Jesse Hutchinson, Jr., and was dedicated to Frederick Douglass, whom Hutchinson called "a graduate of the peculiar institution." Someone must have called slavery a "peculiar institution," because I had read that phrase offtimes in the good Father's newspapers.

After a while Goshen began to walk a little and eat on the beach with us at night, but he didn't want to lead anymore. "You doing good, Moses," he said. "Keep leading the meetings." It was really quite simple, I had discovered, if I let other people do the talking.

Still I worried about him. I had seen people die after they seemed to get well. Smallpox started with fever. A week later people felt better as the pox rash broke out in their mouths and on faces, arms, and chests. But the fever returned worse, and some people died on the ninth to fourteenth day as the pox sores ran with pus. Some illnesses were more severe than others.

Goshen's pox rash began to dry and crust over. The spots were light pink sores on brown skin. He looked awful. I was glad he couldn't see himself, as he was most careful and refined about his appearance. After five or six weeks, scabs fell off people, leaving pox-pitted skins.

I had no idea why I hadn't come down with malaria or smallpox. Sarah said, "Moses, you meant by God to lead us. That's why he ain't called you into fever suffering."

I suppose there was some reason.

One morning during meeting, Rusty Rich stood with a long plaited vine in his hands. He shouted, "I say we give that Mr. Kock a flogging!" and he snapped the whip.

I grew quite anxious, but Goshen, sitting at my feet, squeezed my ankle.

"What do you think?" I asked as usual after a suggestion.

"Yeah, he brought us here with no provisions."

"Not on the boat!" someone shouted.

"Not on the island!"

"He's a murderer of our people!" another called.

The shouting grew louder and louder. I felt things were getting out of control, but Goshen kept a steady pressure on my ankle.

Robert the Preacher finally stood and said, "Vengeance is mine, saith the Lord!" He sat down.

"If Mr. Kock's a dirty dog, should we become like him?" someone ventured.

That didn't make sense to me at the time; I was worried that Mr. Kock would overhear. If we survived and were reported, we could be killed for mutiny or some such thing.

"Lie down with dogs, rise up with fleas," another said.

Goshen finally stood and slowly stripped his shirt and undershirt off. His back was a torrent of crisscrossing, raised scars. "Am I a man who knows the whip?" he asked, turning his back for all to see. He walked among them.

People murmured.

"And yet," he said, turning slowly to face them, "I would not that any human be submitted to flogging."

Why hadn't he done that sooner! He let all those people shout and scream for ages, and then he stopped it. His words were followed by what-if whisperings and laughter. And then I saw: people had needed a time to explode, to say what they felt. I wished I knew and understood as much as Goshen.

We hadn't had rain for days. Remembering what Jack said, I draped canvas like a funnel around our water barrel to help fill it when it rained. On cloudy days I watched dark nimbostratus clouds rain out to sea. By the time they reached Cow Island, we only had a misting. I was angry because the sea stole our rain.

We buried five more people, three of them women, dead from malaria following smallpox, and Rusty Rich was one of the two men. Life on the island was growing more and more intolerable for everyone.

When Goshen was strong enough, we walked to the north side of the island again. Hugging his knees, Goshen sat against a big rock in good hot shade. I sat cross-legged on top of that rock and stared and stared across that water to Hayti.

"Goshen, I could never swim that far."

"Might be that it's so shallow you could walk partway."

That was dreaming of Christmas angels. "But, Goshen, even if I perchance could swim, sharks would eat me."

"Might be that you splash a lot and scare them."

"Goshen, I had a shark after me when I was fishing. They don't scare easy." That very morning I had seen a shark as Goshen stood beside me with a newly woven basket while I caught fourteen good-size fish. Among us we had basket weavers and mat weavers. By now we all slept on handsome woven mats.

"Might be you could take a raft."

"No trees big enough to tie together." But fern trees?

Most people slept now in round homes with branches of giant fern trees as roofs and thin, reedlike branches making the airy, circular walls. The roofs extended far enough to give shade around the homes. Homes were in clusters facing central spaces and looked like villages.

Goshen asked, "Might be that you could float there?"

"Goshen," I said, "would that water barrel float?"

He clapped. "I knew you'd find a way. Yes! And give you distance from the shark."

Gift of angels. Distance from the shark!

14

No sooner had we decided to use the empty barrel, than the first good rains fell. Cumulonimbus clouds with pale gray undersides gave us a soaking as we walked back. Would people let us take the barrel now?

We always ate supper on the beach after sunset. For supper that night we ate tasty smoked fish. We each had a pint-size seashell of clear fresh rainwater. How sweet it tasted.

Goshen felt his way from group to group, and in each he squatted and explained our plan. I heard wrangling. Some testy people had begun to argue from dawn to dusk; others discussed and laughed.

Hardships challenge people to rise or to fall in the virtues of patience and industry and sharing. Most of our people ended virtuous and hopeful. However, they debated everything. For former slaves I suppose it was a taste of freedom to discuss things at length.

"That barrel is for our water supply," they said.

"We'll lose our water barrel and Moses too. What's to keep him from blowing out to sea?" someone else asked.

I hadn't thought of that. I needed a way to guide myself.

"Sharks will drag him off it."

"He'll never make it. I seen that distance. He'll dry up in the sun."

That was something to think about as well. It was so hot, we each had to sip a heap of sandy water in the day. How would I manage floating on a barrel in full hot sunlight?

Sarah wept. She plowed weakly through the fine white sand, knelt, and hugged me, rocking back and forth. If Goshen could have seen her, he would have been jealous. He liked her, but she paid no attention to any man. All she talked about was getting home to Virginia. Now she was most worried for me.

One man told Goshen, "I'll think hard on it."

A woman walked over and patted me on the shoulder. "There's some mule-headed men hereabouts, Moses. Don't let them worry you none." I thanked her.

For two days they debated. The next evening Mr. Kock called me over. I thought sure he would ask about the plans.

"How much is cotton bringing for the bale, Moses?"

"I don't know, sir."

He wore his derby and sat chest deep in water. Wet clothes kept him cool, I suppose. Besides, he sat in the shade of the mangrove trees, moving as the sun moved.

"Are they picking cotton, Moses?"

"Yes, sir. I mean, no, sir."

"That's good. Are the crops good?"

"I don't know, sir." I kept getting confused, but it mattered little what I said.

"Moses, keep your spirits high. I'm governor of Isle à Vache. I'm sure this colony will surprise them all."

"Yes, sir." Mr. Kock hadn't heard any of our loud arguments. The water barrel question was safely in our hands.

A friend of Jacob wove several fern branches into two broad, flat oars. The oars were light but strong, and pushed water quite well.

"Goshen," I said, "these are my oars." We were sitting with several men on rocks looking across at Hayti.

Smiling, he ran his hands over them. "Good, good."

"Some men have floated wood out and watched from the hillside," Jacob said. "There's a current flows around that arm of Hayti."

"Don't you use any strength to row when you don't need to," Goshen told me. "Float as far as you can. And remember, wherever you touch land, you can walk from there."

I nodded. Why me? I thought. Why couldn't I have come down with smallpox or malaria? Or even a simple snakebite? I looked around. How about a scorpion bite? I sighed.

Goshen heard my sigh and patted my back. "I'll be watching with the men right up there on the hillside."

Sure, I thought, when the shark snatches me off the barrel, they'll tell you. I felt pretty sour but I said, "I'll wave."

Somehow I thought of Aunt Rebekah lying on that bench with all the candles burning. Had Father wondered when I wasn't there the next morning? I always brought him coffee and opened the drapes. How did he discover Rebekah? I'm sure the candles were still burning.

Aunt Rebekah! How I missed her. Remembering her made me feel guilty. What would I do in life, when and if I escaped this island? I must needs think on that!

Goshen and Jacob were asking for a big shell to fill with water for me to take. Some men rolled the barrel down to that northern shore of Cow Island. I pushed it into the water.

The water barrel rolled over and over and began to sink.

"The spigot's open," someone called.

A group of men hauled it back. They put a seal on the spigot and stuffed leaves around the top to make it stay on.

I tried to ride it again. When it rolled, I fell off and struck my head on a rock. Besides a headache, I had new knowledge: my legs dangled far enough down for some shark to bite off.

"Might be that water in it would keep it from rolling," said Goshen.

"And it must needs float with the spigot topside," someone said.

I let someone else try it with seawater inside. I covered my hurting head with cool, damp seaweed and lay in the shade, listening to them.

When I woke up many hours later, the barrel had thin stripped branches bound across it, front and back, extending six feet out on either side. Those branches were tied to others parallel to the barrel. Those parallel branches carried empty yellow gourds as floats. I had woven mats on which to rest my feet, and Y-shaped branches on which to rest my oars.

Now the barrel rode the waves without rolling. The men pulled it in.

"Make the vines fast," Goshen said, running his hands around the barrel. He tugged the floats off and ripped the vines loose.

Men shouted angrily: "Why you do that, Goshen? We fixing to make this work, and you studying to break it up!"

"Blind man ordering us like as though he was a boss man!"

"Make them fast," he repeated. "I don't want them to come off for the boy halfway over."

They tested vines for the barrel and plaited stronger ones with sailor's knots for attaching the branches. They secured the gourds better also, but the outstretched branches alone kept the barrel steady. The barrel seemed seaworthy now, as they used to say in Maryland.

"Now you got you a double outrigger," said Jacob's friend. "Won't nothing turn that barrel over. Sailors from the South Pacific taught me about outriggers."

I was constantly astonished at how intelligent these people were. They had great learning that wasn't from books. I suppose human intelligence belongs to all regardless of position in life.

There were comments of "could be," "should of went here," and "Lord help him." I felt dizzy, and I hadn't eaten all day.

"He'll leave first thing in the morning," Goshen said.

They hauled stones to hold the barrel where it couldn't

roll or blow away. With Goshen's hand on my shoulder, I walked behind the group of excited men crossing the island to our camp.

Sarah met us. "We fixing smoked fish special for supper," she said, holding my hand. Other women hugged me.

People said, "Moses, we praying for you."

As I ate by the sea, everyone looked over my way. Talk was lively. Some men were placing bets:

"I bet you two days' fishing he won't make it."

"Over and back. I'll bet three cups of water."

"My water? No, you ain't stealing my water."

"Next rain?"

"Five days' cleaning fish, he make it safe."

"Over and back?"

"Well, over. Don't think we'll ever see the likes of him again."

I ate slowly and all alone. Goshen was discussing the plan with people. Two women said it was the same as murder. Goshen explained things to them.

He was led over and said, "Moz, we thinking you should leave off farther east up the island. Then the current carry you back down to that jutted-out part of Hayti."

I nodded and said, "Yes."

They started to lead Goshen away.

The moon was full. The black sky was clear of clouds and sprinkled with stars piercing the darkness.

I was thinking hard on the trip, working out problems for myself. Aunt Rebekah would have liked that.

Nights always cooled off. As soon as the sun set, the

heat lifted, and the sea grew calm. No sun. No heat. Calm
sea.

"Goshen," I called jumping up, "night is the time to
leave. My spirits are high, and I feel ready. I'll leave
tonight!"

15

Everyone who could walk, and some who couldn't and who weakly leaned on others, crossed the island to launch me and my barrel. About twelve were too ill with smallpox or malaria to come along. I sensed that this was the most exciting thing to happen since we landed. It was like a night of jubilee. As we crossed the rocks, one by one they walked up and placed a hand on my head in blessing.

"Moses, may the good Lord watch between thee and me whilst we are apart."

"I hope thee and me meet on earth again, Moses."

"Have a safe trip and a gladsome return, Moses."

"Moses, may the good Lord take a liking to thee."

Tears smarted my eyes. I felt trembly in the legs, and I could hardly breathe. For some reason I had put my shoes on. Maybe I thought they would protect my feet from shark bite. I had napped that afternoon while people prepared my barrel, so I didn't feel sleepy. It would be most dangerous to get sleepy and tumble into the sea.

Goshen swung a large pointed snail shell full of fresh water over my shoulder. It was held by braided vines as a strap. The vines were wrapped around the quart-size shell to hold it upright. I could also set the shell in a space on the foot mat.

Men had tied vines, twisted and knotted, for me to hold to keep me on the barrel. My barrel-boat was launched lengthwise, and I sat up holding vines like riding a horse with reins. Still, those wonderful mats on each side were all that was between my feet and a shark's mouth.

Men waded out, pushing the water barrel in shallow water. Swaying but steady, the barrel-boat came alive. Goshen tried to follow, but he kept stumbling in holes and nobody was helping him. When I saw him stop, I called, "Good-bye, Goshen."

From the corner of my eye I saw him wave. Many lessons had I learned from him, besides the lesson of our worth.

I thought of my bread he had hidden in his leather pouch long ago, the bread he had given to Sarah on board. Between my undershirt and my outer shirt, I had fresh leaves and several dried fish. I was prepared in ways I had learned from him, but for what?

One by one the men turned back. Now the sea was chest high to most of them, and the coral bottom was uneven.

"Good-bye," I called.

The barrel swung around when they let go, and I saw all our people on the side of the hill. I waved. By the full moon I saw them all waving back. Over lapping waves I heard them singing. Standing there they looked so few.

Goshen and I had figured that more than seventy people had already died, on the voyage and since landing. I remembered many faces and missed them. The shoreline of the island now had a double row of graves with headstones. Burials were almost daily.

Getting help was most necessary, and it was up to me.

When the men turned back, in truth, I felt panic. I wanted to whine like a puppy and frantically paddle toward them. But if ever I had an important job to do, this was it. Worth more than eight hundred dollars!

Although my face was wet with tears, I smiled at my foolishness. Goshen had taught me that we are people of immeasurable worth just from *being*, and as beings we have work to do, a role to play. Herein was my work, my role for the moment.

Just to try out the oars, I began to row. It felt good. The farther out onto the sea I went, the cooler it seemed. Refreshing. For some time I rowed while a cloud covered the moon. When I glanced up, I saw I had turned around. I was rowing back toward our island. Did the people on the hillside notice? Did they tell Goshen? I felt foolish and embarrassed.

After that I sighted by some stars and the moon's glow. About a mile out I got caught in that current. It was swift, pulling my barrel on a course between the islands. I rested.

Fish jump at night. I passed through a school of leaping fish. One silver-blue shiny fish flapped briefly on the barrel.

My barrel-boat needed a name. I had never learned the name of the ship that brought us there. When we were leaving I had meant to read on the side, but the sick people distracted me. I named my barrel-boat *Land of Goshen*. I once knew an old woman, a friend of Rebekah's, who used to say, "Land o' Goshen!"

When I seemed as far from one shore as the other, I began rowing again, but I became thirsty and shifted to drink. I managed the shell, but when I reached in my shirt for bird leaves, one oar slid out of its Y-shaped holder.

The oar shimmied on the surface of the water. It was right alongside of me. In my mind I heard Goshen say, "Might be you can grab it, Moses." I reached over slowly, then tried to grab it. A large animal, in truth big, small eye in huge head, snatched it down. Using the vines, I barely managed to drag myself back on the barrel. Now I only had one oar.

My heart was pounding and, notwithstanding the coolness, I was sweating. I was standing in the need of prayer. After I bent my head and talked to the Lord, my job became more clear.

If I rowed with one oar, I spun around. To go forward, I had to dip on one side then quickly on the other. That was more work, yet it must be done. I rowed rapidly to move across the current and closer to Hayti. Unless I crossed that current, I would end up out at sea somewhere.

From then on I rowed steadily. My arms grew numb with hurt and my back was aching from my seat to my skull. But by rowing constantly I caught the last mangrove root of the island where Hayti was. Seconds later I would have been out to sea and headed for Florida, surely a hundred miles or more away.

I dragged my barrel behind me, clumsy with the double outrigger, and secured it in between trees. Then I bowed my head and gave thanks. I had made it safely. Sipping from my water shell, I rested. Later I found a knobby perch among roots and land, and I fell asleep therein.

The next morning, looking from Hayti, Cow Island shimmered in the sunrise like an emerald with a diamond tip. I yearned to be back and talk to Goshen. Had they been able to see me all the way? Did Goshen know I had made the trip safely? I tied my oar down, and ate my fish. After I found a giant fern tree, I tried to make a second oar.

All day I spent trying to weave that oar together. Jacob's friend was an outstanding basketmaker. His oar was woven and tucked and trimmed most expertly. My efforts were clumsy.

Toward evening I sharpened a stick with the knife Jack gave me. With the stick I speared a nice-size fish and ate it raw. The juices helped my thirst, but I was frightened when a small fish bone got stuck in my throat for a while. My water had long since given out and I must needs suck from a sand pool.

The second night I slept better. The next morning I finished an oar that was fair to middling in quality, tied it to the *Land of Goshen*, and climbed uphill to find a city. After a while I found a colorful shanty made of woven mats.

When I found a lady farming nearby, I asked, "Excuse me, but can you tell me where the mayor is?"

She chattered in French.

I repeated in poor French: *"Pardonnez moi, mais où est le mayor?"*

People laughed at my French. They stared at my sliced-up shoes and salty-gray clothes. The first lady gave me a chunk of bread and filled my shell with sweet water. I chewed and chewed and felt as if I must needs weep out of thankfulness. Perchance I could take some bread back to Goshen.

For two hours as I walked people pointed the way. They spoke faster and different from my French, but they passed me on. Much of the way was uphill, a hard climb with no clear path through the rocks. I kept glancing back, trying to remember houses and turns. I mustn't get lost from *Land of Goshen*.

Finally I came to homes more closely built, and then to a plaza with a stone church and a stone civic building facing each other across a stone paved court. Outside, officials in uniforms stared at me.

I repeated, *"Pardonnez moi, mais où est le mayor?"*

Someone came out of the civic building, grabbed my shoulder as if I were a common criminal, and roughly pulled me inside. I sat in a chair at a table, a real wooden table with what seemed like a hundred years of pits and scratches. Very politely I asked for someone to help us. In French I told them:

"We are on Isle à Vache. We are dying from malaria and smallpox. Please tell our President Abraham Lincoln to send a boat to take us back to America."

Perchance for hours people walked in, people walked out. A frowning man with a gun stood behind me with his arms folded. When I needed to relieve myself, he took me to a latrine, and brought me back. I stared at his long dangling keys.

At least two dozen men had heard my story. The small

stone-face room was unbearably hot. I saw bloodstains on the walls, and chains hung from the back of my chair. It seemed this was an interrogation room for prisoners. Light peeped in through three small windows high in the walls, and there was a wooden bench with a filthy pad on it.

I longed to go down to the shore and cool off in the sea, to be anywhere but in that dark dank room.

At long last a woman brought black beans and rice and bread. The beans were seasoned with chunks of salt pork; the platter of food was delicious. My innards were most gladsome, especially when I was also given a pitcher of cool water and a clay cup.

After I repeated my request one last time, they locked me in the room for the night. The lock was rusted, and the key stuck there. I watched the guard turn the creaking lock, then jerk the key free. I was watching because by this time I was ready to run away. These people wouldn't keep me forever! As soon as I let the right person know, I must needs escape this prison.

I lay on the floor and cried myself to sleep. This was an injustice. Unfair. They wouldn't answer me. Did anyone believe me? All someone had to say was, *"Oui."* "Yes. We'll send a message." Would anyone help us?

16

The next morning I ate eggs and a green vegetable cooked together. My innards danced for joy. I tucked a piece of bread inside my shirt with the dried fish. Several men returned, and I stared at one of them for a few moments.

I jumped up. "You were at our clipper," I called, pointing to him. "You spoke English." I was sure it was one of the men who followed Mr. Kock in their Haytian boat.

The guard snatched me back and lifted a baton to strike me.

"*Non,*" said the official. The guard lowered the stick.

"So," said the man, "Governor Kock's colony has ended in failure." The smiling official placed hands palms down on the table. From his face I sensed no sympathy or understanding.

"Yes, sir," I said, but I felt indignant. In truth we were a success, I was thinking. Working together, we had built homes; we were a community of caring people. We sang in Sunday worship; we fished and survived against daily odds; and we were gleeful as a people in supper celebrations and eventide.

I did not tell him that.

"Over seventy people have died," I said. "We brought smallpox off the clipper, and some people have died of malaria. There was no water for farming."

The man laughed. "Oh, your Governor Kock, he said he would form the world's most successful black society." The man walked back and forth smiling, hands clasped behind his back. "What made that liar seek our island? He told people he had a lease. He dared call himself governor of one of our islands!" The official rubbed his hands and smiled. He turned to me.

"Only seventy dead?" he asked. "I thought you would all be dead by now. I suppose the rain has kept you in water." He rubbed his hands and clasped them behind his back again.

What rain? I thought. We learned to suck water from pools in the sand. We dug and maintained wells. But I must needs keep those things from this angry man who might be our means of escape from the island.

"Please, sir," I said. "Send word to our President Lincoln and his most honorable Congress to send a boat to take us back."

The man seemed not to hear me. Pointing to the guard, he ordered me locked in the room again.

That day was unbearable, but I spent it studying the prison. The room had three windows, but they were high and I had no means of reaching them. The door had a space with bars, but the bars were narrow and strong. I did notice that the door didn't always close shut. When the guard wasn't looking, I jammed a piece of my dry fish in the lock.

When a lady brought me food in the evening, I asked

for five little loaves of bread. I told her how tasty they were. They were no longer than a man's hand, and half as wide. She winked and nodded. Would she suspect that I was trying to escape?

People seemed to understand my French better than I could understand theirs. I spoke word by word and they spoke their words rapidly and all together.

An hour or so later, at sunset, the lady brought me five warm little loaves. The guard dismissed her, closed the door, and left for the night. He thought he locked it, but my fish caught in the slot. The key only partly turned, and I used my knife to twist it open. If there were no outside guard, I perchance could escape.

I hid the loaves safely in my shirt. As soon as it seemed quiet, I jerked the rusty door open and peeked. No one was guarding. No one was looking.

Carefully I slipped out, closed the door, and hid in a flowering bush outside. A few people strolled by. When my heart had stopped hammering my ribs, and I could breathe the cool fresh air calmly, I ran.

Once among trees, I tried to retrace my steps. I walked behind houses in the brush, then slid down the rocks, which was much faster. Perchance people noticed me, but no one stopped me.

"*Bon soir*," they called cheerfully.

I waved rather than spoke. I was afraid my French would give me away.

This time the trip was faster. Climbing uphill had been slow, and I had stopped to talk to people, but now I was going downhill all the way. I heard a gurgling sound and found a splashing stream. The water was fresh and cool, so I undressed and bathed by moonlight, then dressed and filled my shell. It seemed a short time before I reached my barrel-boat. I had remembered the way, and I was ready to leave.

So ready was I that tears came when I realized that I could not leave from there. From that spot I would be carried out to sea. I must needs drag the barrel and outrigger branches along the shoreline east to a spot where the current would carry me home as I rowed across.

Notwithstanding my disappointment, I was feeling strong and refreshed. I walked ahead of the outrigger branches, dragging the barrel by plaited knotted vines. Along water with a sandy bottom I walked rapidly, but ofttimes I had to climb on sharp coral. There I was pleased to have my squishing shoes to protect my feet. By the time I reached a position far enough east to flow and row back, I saw a whisper of light break quickly into a concert of sunrise. I do believe, in truth, that it was the most beautiful sunrise I ever saw before or after.

The sun seemed propelled by fingers of pink pushing it up out of the sea. A cloudless sky was brightened further by birdsong behind me. Those birds sang a morning song of praise.

All alone, I hid my barrel and branches among rocks and crouched in a crevice of stone near another tiny stream. No fish were in the stream that washed out to the sea. I used Jack's knife and sharpened another stick, but I was not successful in spearing a fish from the shoreline.

Instead, I opened shells and hooked out snails. To write about it now, it seems intolerable, but I ate the slippery snails raw. Why had we overlooked snails for food on Cow Island?

In the afternoon there was a shower. I kept my five loaves dry under a rock. Nightfall was clear and calm, with a diminished moon draping herself in clouds like a slave child in tattered clothing.

I pushed out and climbed aboard my *Land of Goshen*. After a prayer, I began rowing with both oars. This time I was careful to hold on to them. One mat was loose, and it flapped around. When I reached the middle of the current, I rested for only a moment. The time on Hayti had healed my sore muscles. Now I felt some aches, but my spirits were high because I would be back on Cow Island soon.

Something bumped my barrel-boat. I felt the barrel and outrigger rise and plop back on the water. Beside me, a smooth dark head rose to look at me with a small button-eye. Soon there were dark backs rising all around me, button-eyes staring.

It behooved me to stop rowing. I think this was the animal that dragged my oar below on the first crossing. Perchance they liked its taste? I hugged my oars across my chest and stared all around me. I was thrilled at such high adventure.

The animals, small whales or dolphins or something else, seemed friendly. They kept bumping the barrel. With each bump the starboard outrigger grew looser. Lord, I prayed, let those branches remain fast. Without them the *Land of Goshen* would roll, roll me down to the deep.

I couldn't row, and I was drifting in the current farther and farther along Cow Island. Aunt Rebekah, send those Christmas angels!

As quickly as they appeared, my sea animal friends departed. I began rowing frantically then, and successfully crossed the current. When my arms pained into my shoulders, I rested. Knowing where I was going made the trip seem shorter. I could see the coral reef. I secured my loaves of bread on top of the barrel and slipped off to test how close the reef was. The water was only shoulder high, and refreshingly cool.

Walking behind the outrigger branches, I pushed the *Land of Goshen* ahead of me. My landing on Cow Island was far below the spot where I had launched. No one was around, so all alone I dragged the barrel and branches on shore and stored it fast thereon.

The night was cool and half-finished by the time I set off to cross the island. As I grew closer to my friends, I smelled the smoked fish they had had for dinner. I began to run and skip. Goshen was sleeping in his woven home.

"Goshen," I whispered, "wake up!"

"What? It's a dream?"

"It's me. I'm back. I did my best, Goshen."

He leaped up and hugged me. When he started to shout, I covered his lips. "Wait."

I handed him a loaf of bread. He sniffed it, and squeezed it, and stroked it. "Oh, Moses, bread!"

"It's brown and chewy. I have five loaves: one for Sarah, one for Cassius, one for Simeon. One for each of us."

He reached for his shirt. "We'll go for them," he said. We went through the woods to the clearing where they lived.

Five fishes had started our crowd of strangers to becoming a family. Now, it seemed to me, we united our small family group with a meal of five loaves of rough-grained, chewy bread.

The five of us whispered and laughed. They hugged me over and over. I ate that bread with reverence.

"You come back," Cassius said. "I thought Jacob and his friend had sent you into the hands of death."

"I told the Haytians," I said. "I even saw an official who was on the boat following Mr. Kock that day."

"What they tell you?" Sarah asked. "When we going home to Virginia?" She had hugged Goshen as well as me, and he grinned from east to west.

I sighed. "In truth, they promised nothing. But they know we need help. I asked them to get word to our president."

"How long will that take?" Simeon asked.

Cassius said, "You know how long it taken us to get here. A boat has gotta go and ask to send a boat back." He shook his head. With the back of his hand he wiped bread crumbs off his lips, and he said, "I'd keep fishing."

The next morning people shouted, "Praise the Lord!" Again I was hugged and kissed. Some men picked me up and carried me in procession on the beach with a line of people clapping and shouting and singing and swaying behind us. Leaning down, I thanked Jacob and his friend.

"The oars were great," I said. "And the floats really lasted." Finally they put me down.

Over and over I told them about the homes on Hayti, the prison room, the food—except for the loaves I secretly brought back—the officials, the door stuck open with dry fish.

"Praise the Lord," people called.

"Hallelujah," they sang.

Talking to different groups, I saw my Negro race in a clear light. What a beautiful people we were. We were a forgiving family, a caring laughing family. Three hundred some people were gentle with one another, and caring for Mr. Kock, notwithstanding that he caused our hardships.

Women were strong, and men respected women. They gave them food first. They repaired women's homes where the women stayed clustered together near the sick. And I felt as if I had hundreds of fathers and mothers. As the youngest, I was everyone's son.

While we were talking on the beach that glorious morning, Mr. Kock walked out of the woods. "Moses," he called.

Slowly I plowed through sand toward him. My wet shoes were heavy with sand, and I felt tired at long last. "Yes, sir."

"Why are the colonists celebrating? Is the cotton picked?"

Poor man. What could I say? "No, sir."

"That's good. Tell them not to lose any in the ginning."

To gin cotton is to pick seeds out of the bolls. Cotton

grows from early spring until late summer and fall before it's picked, I think. Poor Mr. Kock was really confused to think we had a crop ready for ginning in only about seven weeks.

Our self-proclaimed governor strutted away in the sand.

If I hadn't been so angry, I could have pitied Mr. Kock for his foolishness and greed. He had caused great suffering among us, and still some of us survived. At that moment I heard the people singing, "Taste and See the Goodness of the Lord."

Walking out to fish beside Goshen, I suddenly clapped and laughed. "What's happened, Moses? What do you see?"

"Goshen," I said. "At the moment I realize that I love being colored, being a Negro. We're an astonishing people!"

"Amen!" And Goshen grinned.

Two weeks or so later we heard a shout. When we ran to our southern shoreline, I saw a large ship with the Stars and Stripes flying. How had they come so soon?

Jacob ran to me. "Moses, how did this happen?"

Cassius and Simeon and Sarah ran over.

Mouth open, I raised both hands.

People were yelling and gathering their few treasures: rosy seashells, wood carvings, hair combs of spiny sea skeletons. I treasured my pointed water shell and my shoes.

"I don't know," I told Jacob. "Maybe they had written our government before I got there. Or maybe they had a fast boat."

"No, 'tain't true," Sarah said, hugging me. "You made this here boat come for us."

We had been on the island about seven weeks.

Hands behind his back, Mr. Kock met the first rowboat. "Tell your captain my colonists are ready for transport," he said. "They deserve a rest. Board them carefully. We have completed a successful colony. My workers have bales of cotton ready to take to market." Barefoot, but wearing wet coat and derby, Mr. Kock was the first to leave.

Jacob led us singing, "We are Climbing Jacob's Ladder," as boats carried our friends out to the government-chartered ship. Across the sea, I could hear the singing of people on rowboats grown faint and out of tune with our singing. At the end, Cassius, Simeon, Sarah, Goshen, and I went with ten people shivering from malaria chills despite the heat.

Our death toll on shore was fifty-five. I heard people arguing that counting those thrown overboard on the first days, the hand of death had taken almost a hundred, about forty on board and fifty-five on shore. Graves on shore were easy to count, but later I was sorry I hadn't kept records of names. About three hundred boarded the ship.

Unlike our clipper ship, which had three tall masts and jibs, this ship was a paddle-wheel steamer with only two masts and jibs. Tall stacks carried off smoke, and the engine and paddle wheels made a constant friendly rumble. What a sweet sound when it was taking us home fast!

Our trip home began pleasantly. Doctors gave quinine to our people who were sick with malaria. Smallpox patients slept in a quarantined room. There were mattress pads for everyone, and Goshen and I took ours and slept by the warm smokestack.

Some way, Mr. Kock found shoes. Perchance they were in his sea trunks. Heels clicking, he strutted up and down the boat's upper deck. I heard the captain tell Mr. Kock that we colonists would all go to a camp in Virginia.

I passed word about Virginia across the boat to Sarah, and watched her dance, then kneel and fold her hands. When I described it to Goshen, he laughed. We were both most pleased for her.

I began to think. Virginia had been a slave state like Maryland, but it had broken away from the Union. Maryland was still in the Union. Neither was good for me. I wanted schooling. I had to make a good life for myself, and I thought I knew what I wanted to study.

According to what I overheard from the captain, soldiers were still fighting the War Between the States. The captain told Mr. Kock that the Union was ahead in recent battles. That was good. The slaveholding South was not winning. Mr. Kock didn't seem to really hear him.

"Did you bring the cotton on board?" he asked.

"No, sir. No one seemed to know about your cotton, Governor."

Mr. Kock raised a hand. "Thousands of bales, all ginned. I remember the night they ginned it. You must have it below. That's good, Captain." He straightened his shoulders proudly and marched away.

"Governor," the captain called, "I just told you I haven't seen your cotton." The captain stared after Mr. Kock. He must have wondered by what magic we grew, chopped, and picked cotton in just seven weeks.

18

While the captain and Mr. Kock were talking on deck, Goshen and I overheard the sailors. They discussed us while we were standing not three feet away.

"Don't they look like savages?" one sailor asked.

"Yes," his friend said, "ragged, ugly, and black. I can't stand the sight of Negroes."

"I hear they killed one another."

"A hundred dead."

"Probably ate the dead."

"They're cannibals, all of them. As soon as whites ain't keeping them servile, they return to heathen ways. I tell you, Lincoln has loosed savages on us all."

The first sailor laughed. "All those men and only eight women. You know that was a wild time."

"Savages," his friend said, shaking his head.

I felt so sad, my throat was choked. I walked away.

Across the ship an hour later one sailor asked another: "Did you hear that they ate their dead? They tell me they were cannibals. And the women. Only eight women for three hundred men." He laughed and looked at me with a curled lip.

By the steam engine room two sailors spit on Goshen and said, "Take that, you heathen."

"Goshen," I said, pulling him away. "I regret that."

"I know, Moz." He shrugged and sighed. "Now we are going back home where there's slavery, and whites who think we're ugly and dumb."

I leaned against the railing of the quarterdeck and stared at the sky. I felt sadness drape over me like a dead man's shroud. Because of Goshen's interest, I remembered our women. So many had died. I saw their pretty faces as I stared at the clouds. Cumulus clouds in fluffy white were forming, growing, breaking up. The puffs were all leaning backward. "Why are the clouds leaning backward, Goshen?"

He smiled. "I hear clouds tilt in the trade winds, Moz."

"Goshen?"

"Yes, Moz."

"Goshen, my name is Moses. I hate it when you call me Moz."

"Why didn't you inform me earlier? Moses, I'll remember that."

"Thank you, Goshen. And you understand this: I won't let what others think about us colored bother me much. I understand about human weakness more. And I respect myself for who I am."

"Good for you, Moses." His voice was low.

With every hour the air grew colder. I began shivering. Sailors passed out narrow navy blankets and everyone walked the decks wrapped in scratchy, dark blue wool.

The cold seemed unbelievable. "We left in winter, had summer, but we returning in the same winter," Jacob said.

121

"Still cold in the United Sates, Moses. Ain't that something?" Sarah said. We stood looking out to sea.

"I know," I told her. "Seems we were away so long, but we're returning to cold weather still."

That evening below deck I overheard the ship's captain tell his first mate: "There's a story we heard from the Haytians, they're all black liars, you know. But they told us a boy named Moses swam six miles in shark-infested waters from Cow Island to Hayti."

"People all have their fantasies." The mate wiped a smile. "Let's ask this boy."

He called me over. Goshen followed, hand on my shoulder. We had mastered the rolling walk on board ship again.

"What's your name, boy?" the captain shouted. Did he think I was deaf? His face was grinning, but he wrinkled his nose at me as if I smelled bad. This time I didn't.

Should I tell him my name? Would he believe anything good? "Christmas, sir." That was true.

"And your name?" He pointed to Goshen, who couldn't see. I signaled by lifting my shoulder.

"Uh, Goshen."

"I see. Goshen and Christmas. Go back to your places."

They chuckled as we boat-walked back.

Sarah passed word of the story among us, and we all laughed in delight. They loved that I told them my name was Christmas.

Now I understood the Haytians. No wonder they had stared at me. They believed that I swam all that distance? But why did they lock me up? Would I ever understand people?

On this *Marcia C. Day* government-chartered ship they fed us well. Twice a day we ate bowls of soup, or bread, or oatmeal. Not fancy food such as Rebekah cooked for Father Fitzpatrick, but food that tasted royal after raw fish, bird leaves, and sandy sips of water.

On the morning of the twentieth of March 1864 we dropped anchor at Annapolis, Maryland. The trip back took one day less than a week. Besides having speed from steam power, the ship had made no stops.

All of us gathered on the deck and sang, "Praise, Praise the Lord and Thank Him." From singing together at church services and burials, our practiced harmony was sweet to the ear. Even a sailor remarked about our singing.

"Sing well for heathens, don't they?"

"All savages sing well."

Arm in arm and interwoven at the knees, we clung together as we had done during the storm off Isle à Vache. At Sarah's request I began reciting St. John's Prologue. But the sailors began shoving us.

"What are the savages doing?" asked the captain, his voice shrill. He ordered, "Break them up."

Mr. Kock tried to stop them. Batons split some foreheads but we finished and released one another peacefully. The last song Jacob led us in singing was "Nobody Knows the Trouble I Seen." Appropriate.

The ship's doctor cleaned and bandaged the wounded. Why had they been so afraid of people at prayer? That had been a kind of farewell gathering.

Within the hour sailors began rowing boatload after

boatload to the docks, where our people were taken to wagons. Our little family left at the end again, and Cassius, Sarah, Simeon, Goshen, and I were on the same wagon. Side flaps kept the chilly winds out. Most of my friends sat on benches, but I sat on the hard wooden floor of the horse-drawn wagon.

"Moses," Goshen said, "where are you thinking to live?" He called me by my full name after my request. That's to the honor of the kind of person he is.

"Maryland has slavery still," I said. And I thought of Rebekah's Christmas Eve prayer. She understood so much and she wanted me to learn about life. Maybe now I understood more.

"Not Maryland," he said.

"Virginia's free for slaves, but they're at war and seceded from the Union. Of course, Arlington is under Union soldiers."

"Not Virginia," he said.

I said, "In truth the District of Columbia is free for colored and a right goodly place."

"Yes," Goshen said. "Moses, if I'm right, we should be in D.C. shortly. Keep an eye out. Then we'll say good-bye and go seek our fortunes."

I was still dizzy from the ship, my head ached, and I was strangely tired. But I peeped from under the side flaps of the wagon. At long last we were in the city.

"This is it."

Goshen and I bade farewell to our friends—everyone in the wagon.

"You'll see your beloved Virginia again," Goshen told Sarah.

"Moses," Cassius said, "I been thinking that you must needs write our story. You must tell the truth, for those of us living and for those of us dead. President Lincoln and the government will never know the truth from anyone else."

I thought about the sailors' version, Mr. Kock's version. What Cassius said was true. I must needs write this account.

"I promise," I said. I placed my hand on my heart, then raised my hand to the sky for God's help.

We all hugged. When the wagon slowed for a cross street, Goshen and I slipped out the back and walked away quickly.

"Now where do we go?" I asked Goshen. I wanted to avoid the wharf. It was late, and growing dark in the March eventide.

"Why, we're going to find that nice colored lady's boardinghouse," he said. "Do you still have my gold pieces?"

"Be assured I do." We passed several men and women on the street. I looked them over. Who would know the kind of boardinghouse we sought? After a time I saw a colored gentleman who, from his clothing, seemed quite respectable.

"Sir," I said, "we're looking for a boardinghouse. A small one, run by a lady. . . ." I waved my hand as if trying to remember her name.

We must have looked pretty strange. Our clothes were whole but gray from being washed in the sea. Neither of us wore a hat, and we were wrapped in blue blankets.

I had begun to shiver and my throat was painful. With the tip of my tongue, I felt sores in my mouth.

"Oh," the man said, "you mean Miss Phoebe Wilson's house?"

"Yes, sir." Sounded good to me.

He pointed. "She's the next to last house on this block."

Miss Phoebe Wilson answered the door. She carried a candle.

Her straggly brown hair showed pink scalp. Her high yellow skin was covered with ugly pox pits, her brown teeth were twisted, and one brown eye looked south when the other looked west. She was fish-bone thin.

"Good evening," she said in a young, melodious voice. She shielded her candle and smiled, showing those twisted teeth.

"We're looking for room, ma'am. We just docked at Annapolis," I was shaking for some reason. Why wasn't Goshen speaking up?

"Poor boy," she said. She reached and felt my forehead. "You're sick with fever. Come in, come in."

I held out one of Goshen's gold pieces. "Here's pay, ma'am. We need rooms until we can find work."

"I can work on land or sea," said Goshen.

"Come in," she repeated, "I have a room for two at the top of the stairs." She held the candle to my face. "I do believe your son has smallpox, sir. Having suffered the same myself, I'd be pleased to help you."

19

Our room at Miss Phoebe's boardinghouse was large, with fluffy white curtains at front windows overlooking a north west Washington street. Hers was a small boardinghouse, only four other gentlemen and a lady roomed and boarded with her.

We had two dressers, a large wardrobe, and two brass rail beds with real bedsprings and button mattresses. Pretty braided rag rugs lay like house dogs beside our beds. She had made them herself. A hardworking lady, Miss Phoebe baked bread and braided rugs to sell for extra income.

For the first month or two I dozed on and off. Miss Phoebe kept our shades pulled because smallpox made my eyes sensitive to light. Now I sympathized with sick people on the boat and on the island. My case was most severe. Goshen fed and bathed me. He carried me in his arms when I needed the chamber pot. What tender nursing I had. It made up for the nightmares that came with the fever, nightmares of starving, and being whipped, and being lost, and crying for Aunt Rebekah.

Miss Phoebe was a most outstanding cook, on a standing with my beloved Aunt Rebekah. I sipped chicken broth and fish chowders until I could swallow real food. How Miss Phoebe catered to my needs! She cooked tasty food to tempt my appetite.

While recovering I thought about what I wanted for myself in life. As a free American, how could I best serve people? I thought I knew what I was going to do, but I would need schooling.

By mid-May 1864 I was strong enough to sit on the side of my bed, and begin writing this account. Miss Phoebe supplied me with paper and seemed quite impressed at my story. It was slow going as my hand was weak, and my eyes were watery. Now I understood that some people who hadn't worked hard on Cow Island, couldn't work hard. They weren't lazy, they were weak.

By July I was strong enough to go up and down the steps. Since I could stay by myself, Goshen went out seeking employment. Day after day Goshen walked, asking for work. I felt sorry that he wouldn't let me go with him. In spite of his blindness, Goshen was not given to idleness. He inspired me.

For several weeks I wandered slowly in Washington, inquiring about schools that would take a colored boy. Most schools said, "No," outright. They said Congress was considering funding separate public schools for coloreds. However, one high school principal looked over his glasses and asked:

"Are you willing to work?"

"Yes, sir." I was most willing to work for an education.

"If you'll work without pay, I'll take you on. We have a janitor now. You can take his place mopping floors. Listen at the classroom doors, and you can learn plenty."

"Can't I go in the classroom with the other students?"

"Of course not. This high school is for white boys and girls. But I'll allow you to work and listen."

All night I thought about that opportunity. The next morning I declined—mostly because the colored janitor needed that job.

One day a friend who knew me pointed out a lady on a street corner. "Moses," he said, "you looking for to learn? That high-yellow colored lady over there run a school. Ask her."

I ran up to the lady. She looked startled, so I stepped back. "Please, ma'am," I said. "I can read and write quite well, but I need to learn history and geometry and geography and astronomy." Those were the courses taught in high schools I had visited.

She looked me up and down. "Have your parents the money for tuition at my school?"

"No, ma'am," I said, "but I'm capable of working. And I cipher quite well. I know Latin and some French and Spanish."

A carriage drew up at the curb. The lady raised her skirt to step up.

"Please," I said, holding the carriage door, but standing in her way. "None of the high schools will teach me." And I told her about the schools I had visited.

"What is your name, young man?"

"Moses Christmas, ma'am."

"And where do you reside?"

I gave her Miss Phoebe Wilson's address. The lady raised already-arched eyebrows. "With your parents?"

Why was she so concerned about parents? I said, "With a man who is like a father to me. And a lady who is very kind. We board with her."

"I know," she said in a lower voice. "Phoebe Wilson is my cousin. I'll get in touch with you, Moses." She entered the carriage and rode away.

I held my breath. What did that mean? Should I tell Miss Phoebe? I continued visiting schools.

Goshen searched far and wide, and in August he found a job but one block away at a most unusual task for a blind man. After practicing on me and others for a while, he cut gentlemen's hair.

The proprietor allowed that by feeling, Goshen cut hair as well as any sighted barber. Soon clients asked for him.

The money was good—everyone knew barbering was one of the best-paying jobs for a colored man—and Goshen shared half and half with the proprietor. Between customers when work was slow, Goshen could come home.

In the kitchen the night Goshen earned his first week's pay, he was one jubilant colored gentleman. I overheard him.

"What are you doing in my kitchen, Mr. Goshen?" Miss Phoebe asked. From the dining room I saw her wipe her hands.

"I'm here to help, Miss Phoebe." He reached for the dish towel on a rack. She was a most tidy lady and had a place for everything. "When a lady bakes shad and shad roe like that for dinner, a gentleman has to keep her happy."

"Oh, Mr. Goshen."

"Yes, indeed. Miss Phoebe, you're the cream in my coffee. Kindly and good, you are, ma'am. Took me and Moses in when we were standing in the need of help."

"Oh, Mr. Goshen." She twisted her apron, and I watched her dissolve like a teaspoon of sugar in a cup of hot tea.

Goshen dried a dish and laid it down. "Moses knows I'm a hardworking man of honor. And now I'm looking to settle down." He sighed. "I'm weary of being a stranger in strange ports, as they say, ma'am. The War Between the States is still raging, but I'm at peace."

He held out his hand, she put her hand in his, and Goshen kissed her hand. I felt embarrassed.

"I'll be upstairs," I called.

From that day Goshen began serious courting of Miss Phoebe.

When he came to bed late that night, I told him, "Goshen, you never wanted to know if Miss Phoebe was pretty."

"Moses, Moses," he said. "I was so worried that I would lose you with the smallpox, I didn't want to know. You were mighty ill and knocking on death's door. And by the time I could ask you, I knew. She's gladsome pretty, and I don't need anybody to tell me."

"Goshen," I said, "you're right. I think Miss Phoebe is the most beautiful lady ever I have known." In truth, you notice that I said "known" and not "seen."

Goshen laughed and clapped his hands.

Miss Phoebe coming up the stairs with her night lantern called, "Is there anything wrong, gentlemen?"

"No ma'am," we answered. "Nothing at all."

As the days passed, Goshen saved money in his mattress. He gave me money for my own too, and I saved for school.

One morning while I was writing, Miss Phoebe had a visitor. They were downstairs for some length of time, laughing and talking about family. I peeked over the rail and saw it was the lady I had talked to on the street. Educated in Boston, Miss Mathilda Thomas was wealthy and ran a school for colored boys and girls in Washington. Later I learned that she and Miss Phoebe had a grandfather who had been a wealthy white newspaper owner. He had educated and supported his grandchildren.

Goshen took an hour off from work for lunch, and we had just gone up to rest when Miss Phoebe asked to come up.

She introduced all of us.

Miss Mathilda held out a book. "Moses," she said, "can you read this for me?" She held out a primer reader. That was an insult to my ability, but she carried several newspapers in her bag.

"May I read that, ma'am?" I asked. Politely, I hoped.

I picked up the Daily Morning Chronicle and read a column for her. Beyond the Chronicle, which was a Washington, D.C. paper, was an old New York Herald. A front page headline caught my eye, and I called out.

"Goshen, raise the shades. There's news about us!"

Goshen moved smoothly in the house by then. We were both dressed in new clothes he had bought, and of course we had fresh haircuts. When we arrived with long hair, we must have looked wild. No wonder the sailors thought we were savages.

"Here," I called, "listen to this. The headline reads: The Negro Colonization Scheme. It's right here, third column of the first page of the Tuesday March 22, 1864, newspaper." I could hardly believe it. The world knew about us after all! The newspaper was about six months old, but that didn't matter.

"Read it," Goshen said.

Miss Phoebe said to her cousin, "Isn't Moses sweet? He's so excited. I told you he really could read and write, Mathilda."

"Listen," I said. "Messrs. Tuckerman and Forbes, with whom a contract was made for deporting freemen to the island of Avach, the majority of whom had just been brought back by the U.S. government, claim $20,000 amount not payed, and is withheld on grounds that the contract was not fulfilled."

"Avach?" Goshen asked. "They don't even know the name of our island."

"They had the nerve to ask for money, but they didn't get it. They say here that our Congress will probably repeal the appropriation for colonizing colored people. That's good. Now nobody else will be tricked into leaving our country. It's all here in writing, Goshen." I was trembling, but I read further.

"Our secretary of interior is quoted as saying, 'No disposition is manifested by freedmen of the United States to leave the land of their nativity. Time will solve this problem.'"

Goshen nodded. I saw his eyes grow watery.

"Down here it says they employed a German named Kock to superintend. And Goshen, they say, 'Kock neglected to provide properly for their comfort'—for our comfort, Goshen—'either on the voyage out, or to make arrangements for their reception and settlement after their arrival.' It says, 'Consequently they suffered great hardship and some fifty or sixty of them died. The rest were brought back and for the present will be provided for by our government.' They got the number of dead wrong." I took a deep breath. "I wonder who told them that number?"

"And listen, Goshen." I looked up and saw Miss Phoebe smiling at me and nudging her cousin. "It says our friends will join a flourishing colony at Arlington—that's in Virginia, Sarah's Virginia—under Lieutenant Colonel Greene." I put the newspaper down and took a breath.

In my fever, and even in writing the account, I was nagged by the wonder of whether it was all a dream. But it wasn't. How unfair, how unjust! All those freedmen and women who died! We were there, me and Goshen. He had covered his face.

"You poor dears," Miss Phoebe said. "What suffering you've been through. I'll leave you together now, but first Mathilda has something to ask you, Moses."

"Yes, Moses," said Miss Mathilda. "As you know, I run a school for colored boys and girls. I would be willing to extend your schooling for free if you would help me with primary students. I could pay you a weekly sum. Would you like that?"

School? Get some high school learning and maybe be

able to go to college? I had heard of colleges that allowed colored boys to learn. I could earn money, and perchance I could learn about justice from law books.

Surely, now that we were free, colored people would be needing someone to speak up for them. Someone who knew the law.

"Oh, yes, ma'am," I said. "Yes!"

Above my own needs, I would be teaching colored boys and girls to read and to spell and to write. Already I could serve others. I hugged my shoulders for jubilation!

Goshen still covered his face and tears squeezed out from between his fingers.

That fall in October leaving at 4:00 A.M. I began long walks to Miss Mathilda's school. Her classes were held on the first floor of her two-story Washington, D.C., home. Hers was a brick home in a row of houses all alike.

The boys and girls who were my students were most eager to learn. Some had been born of freed parents, others had been slaves like myself. Learning was of high value to them. Some wore patched clothes, but paid their tuition.

Those who were eight or nine sometimes asked, "What can I be now that we're free, Moses? Can we own businesses? Will they let us work at important jobs?" Being from Washington, they thought of being government clerks, postal workers, or political messengers.

My answer was, "Boys and girls, dream high and let us be prepared to fulfill our dreams!"

I was deeply satisfied to be teaching. Already my life had significance, and I was sure that Aunt Rebekah would be pleased. I dared speak to no one of my dream of studying law at Harvard University.

One Sunday in November Goshen hired a horse-drawn cab to carry Miss Phoebe and me with him across the Potomac River to visit Cassius and Simeon and Sarah. It was so good to see them. We hugged and began talking as if we had never parted. Cassius and Simeon were quartered in shabby accommodations in Arlington, and working at packing food for Union soldiers.

Sarah was living with her mother in a wealthy family's home. They were maids. I met her plump smiling mother, Miss Celia. The family was out, so we all had a wonderful meal of ham and collards and potatoes in the kitchen, and laughed about our suppers on the sand. Our cab driver ate with us.

As we prepared to climb into the cab to leave, Sarah whispered, "Seems Goshen is sweet on Miss Phoebe?" I nodded. Sarah hugged me, she was so delighted.

Everyone seemed pleased at how we were doing, though they little knew that at home Goshen and I were both saving: I saved for college, he saved for his own barber business.

Because of weakness I taught three days a week until we celebrated Christmas that year with Miss Phoebe. Goshen gave her a heart-shaped locket, and she embroidered four handkerchiefs for him. I was now fifteen. By January 1865 both the Northern cause of the War Between the States and Moses Christmas were at good strength, and I could help Miss Mathilda five days a week.

Both fall and spring, teaching, and studying history and geography after school took up my weekdays. On Saturdays and Sundays I helped Miss Phoebe, and only in my spare time could I work on this account.

There was a ten o'clock Mass we attended regularly in the basement of a Roman Catholic church. Colored people had Mass in the basement; white people could attend Mass at six, seven-thirty, nine, eleven, or twelve o'clock upstairs in the church proper.

Our Mass was always crowded, so I stood in a corner.

Miss Phoebe told us, "There's an all-colored Catholic church called St. Augustine's. We'll walk there one Sunday."

I was pleased that Miss Phoebe was Catholic like Goshen and myself. We had attended the services on Cow Island, but I had missed our Catholic Mass.

A girl named Leah Lofton brought her little sister to Miss Mathilda's school. I talked to her mornings and afternoons. She was gladsome pretty, and so confused my mind that I wondered if I would be as woman-conscious as Goshen!

On Palm Sunday, which was April 9, 1865, General Lee of the Confederate army surrendered to our General Grant of the Union army. Two days later Goshen and Miss Phoebe and I were among the crowd who heard President Lincoln speak from the balcony of the White House.

I crept near the balcony and heard Senator Harlan ask, "What shall we do with the rebels?"

People in the crowd shouted: "Hang them!" That was a fearful moment. But the president's son Tad, who was a little younger than I, stepped forward and told his father:

"No, no, Papa. Not hang them. Hang on to them."

Our honorable Father Abraham cried out, "That's it! Tad has got it. We must hang on to them."

President Lincoln looked pleased, but seemed greatly worn. The war had aged him since I had seen him and shaken his hand that December day. My hopes of the president reading my account grew stronger. I even planned a meeting on the White House lawn. I would say, "If you please, President Lincoln, read this, my account of Cow Island trickery."

Aunt Rebekah knew Lincoln was a kindly man, concerned about justice, and a lawyer. Perchance he did want colored people to have land on warm islands for our own good. However, as Americans we wanted to work and own land here. Our choice of homeland was a matter of justice.

As a result of hearing President Lincoln give that speech from the balcony, I renamed myself Moses Lincoln Christmas.

Shortly thereafter, on midnight of Good Friday, April 14, 1865, people calling on the Washington street corners passed word that President Abraham Lincoln had been shot attending theater at the Ford. The next morning we heard that he had died.

I felt deeply disturbed. We had lost our kindly president, Aunt Rebekah's Liberator. Now he would never read my story. Easter Sunday I attended Mass with Goshen and Miss Phoebe.

The priest said, "Today we celebrate the Resurrection of Christ from the dead. Although we grieve for our beloved President Lincoln, we have faith in his resurrection too."

His sermon was most consoling. I was no stranger to death. My greatest disappointment was that the president would not read my account. Perchance his cabinet or Congress would.

By the month of May in 1865 I had discovered two city boys named Johnny and Quentin York. They lived across the street from us. They attended school mornings, and worked at a printshop afternoons. I now attended Miss Mathilda's school all day, assisting her primary students as contracted.

Evenings I talked with those boys in a nearby park. Ofttimes when we were sitting on a park bench, they would hit me and run. At first I was disappointed in them, but Goshen talked to me.

"Hit Johnny back."

"But he runs away."

"Run after him. Seems to be playing tag with you, Moses."

I played tag. It seemed foolhardy, but it was fun to chase and be chased in the park. I suppose everything doesn't have to make sense. Ofttimes, however, I ran out of breath. Then I would stretch out on my back on grass and look up at the clouds. One evening I said: "See those clouds, Quentin?" I pointed.

"Right."

"They're nimbostratus. We'll have rain tonight."

"How come you know so much, Moses?"

"Because," I said, "I've been a grown-up all my life, and now at fifteen I'm becoming a boy." Jumping up, I tagged Quentin and ran.

And, oh yes, I now have a button collection. I keep it in my pointed snail shell on my dresser.

On the first Saturday of August 1865 Goshen and Miss Phoebe were married at St. Augustine's Roman Catholic Church. About a hundred people attended the wedding Mass, and we celebrated back at the house.

Cassius, Simeon, Sarah, and her mother, Miss Celia, met us at the church. We were family with a new member in Miss Phoebe.

In a trash heap behind a Washington mansion, I found two books of law: one on British maritime law, and one on contract law. The books were old, but by reading them, already I was a student of jurisprudence.

As for my future, I have no doubt that, God willing, I will one day be a great and noble attorney-at-law, a counselor in justice. And if, perchance, some minor personage should point and say, "That Moses Lincoln Christmas was a leader among savages on Cow Island back in 1864," I will merely smile.

Smile, because I know the truth, and now dearest honorable reader, so do you.

But if another should say, "We indeed read the Cow Island account, and know of deceit perpetrated by that Moses as when he answered questions with Goshen's knowledge, and took credit for it for himself," I shall answer, "Does this imperfection keep me from being an excellent lawyer? Was our honorable President Abraham Lincoln perfect?"

Cow Island: Out of treachery, truth; out of strangers, family; out of struggle, strength; and out of suffering, understanding sweeter than milk and honey in heaven.

✍ Author's Note

As early as 1861 President Abraham Lincoln thought about sending slaves he would free with his Emancipation Proclamation to colonize areas of the world. Abolitionists and freed slaves already violently opposed the plans. However, Lincoln asked Congress for help in removing freed slaves to a "climate congenial to them." He felt that white Americans could not tolerate black Americans living freely among them.

In doing research on Reconstruction, I stumbled upon Lincoln's colonization plans and a Cow Island scheme that involved slaves and freed persons of the District of Columbia leaving from Annapolis, Maryland. I was born and raised in Washington, D.C., and my father's people for several generations came from Washington and Maryland. Since my slave grandparents and their friends might have been involved, I was interested.

After slaves in the District of Columbia were emancipated, Congress appropriated one hundred thousand dollars on April 16, 1862, for colonization. Later in 1862 on July 16, Congress appropriated an additional five hundred thousand dollars with the help of the Midwest Radicals, who were afraid of freed slaves inundating the Midwest.

Lincoln sought advice and treaties with foreign nations for colonies. One area chosen was Chiriquì, near Panama, a part of New Granada (Colombia). Apparently Negro colonists were to mine coal in Chiriquì, but when coal deposits failed scientific tests, the plans for a colony were dropped.

On December 31, 1862, President Lincoln signed a contract with a German businessman named Bernard Kock to colonize five thousand blacks on Isle à Vache, an island two miles wide and eight miles long off southwest Haiti. Isle à Vache, Cow Island—even the name was interesting.

Kock was to be paid fifty dollars a head for all former slaves he removed from the United States. Shortly after signing the contract, on 6 January 1863, Lincoln had second thoughts. He wrote his secretary of state, William H. Seward, and asked him to "retain the instrument under advisement" and not to "countersign the within contract or affix the seal of the United States thereto."

His attorney general, Edward Bates, inquired about Bernard Kock, who called himself "Governor of Isle à Vache, West Indies." Bates advised Lincoln in writing that: "This Governor Kock is an arrogant humbug. He pretends to have a lease of twenty years for Isle aux Vaches." Bates further denounced Kock as a "charlatan adventurer." Bates's opinions are stated in his diary, edited by Howard K. Beale.

I thank the Harold Washington Library's Special Collection, and the Newberry Library, too, in Chicago, for their sources of information.

In a letter Kock asked the United States government for fifty thousand in advance on January 17, 1863, and was apparently refused. So on March 29, 1863, Bernard Kock transferred his contract to Leonard W. Jerome, Henry J. Raymond, Charles K. Tuckerman, Paul S. Forbes, and perhaps others from New York. These men, seeking to profit from such a venture, advanced money for a trial colony.

President Lincoln backed out of the deal. He wrote that he found himself, "moved by considerations by me deemed sufficient," and he authorized Secretary of State Seward to cancel his signature on "sixteenth day of April in the year of our Lord 1863." The collected works of Abraham Lincoln are edited by Roy P. Basler.

Although the contract had been cancelled in the spring of that year, on December 30, 1863, Bernard Kock took more than four hundred former slaves and free-born people of African descent from Washington and Maryland. I suspect Kock planned to establish such an outstanding colony that he would be given the half million in appropriated funds. The colonists left in December and returned three months later in March. Many reasons are given for the failure of the colony.

J.G. Randall's *Lincoln the President* says that the scheme was a failure because of "inadequate planning, want of essentials, poor housing, smallpox, unemployment, cupidity, Haitian opposition, and the strutting unpopularity of Kock." There was also malaria. I read into those words quite an untold story.

Announcing their return, the Tuesday March 22, 1864, *New York Herald* had an article entitled: The Negro Colonization Scheme. I was thrilled to turn the pages of the actual newspaper, thanks to Chicago's Newberry Library.

The paper reported that Messrs. Forbes and Tuckerman of New York had agreed to manage the whole affair. They did not obtain the consent of "Hayti" to their location on the "island of Avach." They employed Bernard Kock to "superintend the enterprise" in spite of the fact that our government "refused to employ him in any capacity."

Apparently there was a holdup in the boatload of former slaves leaving Annapolis, Maryland, and the colonists were only allowed to depart because they were "subjected to real loss and trouble by detention." Could that have been crowding and hunger?

That newspaper article further reported that Kock "neglected to provide properly for their comfort either on the voyage out, or to make arrangements for their reception and settlement after their arrival." Consequently "they suffered great hardships, some fifty or sixty of them died." The number who died varies in different accounts from fifty up to a hundred.

Randall's book says that the *Washington Chronicle* reported when they docked March 20, 1864, "368 colonists returned, about a hundred less than were sent."

They returned to Annapolis, Maryland, on the "government chartered *Marcia C. Day*." The *Washington Chronicle* reported the great joy of the returning survivors, and further remarked on "the folly of attempting to depopulate the country of its valuable labor."

The Tuesday, March 22, 1864, *New York Herald* that I held and read reported that after the colonists returned, Messrs. Tuckerman and Forbes claimed twenty thousand dollars (fifty dollars a head for four hundred people) from our U.S. government. They were not paid, on the grounds that the contract was not fulfilled.

The writer of the article felt that Congress would shortly repeal the appropriation. Remember, this was in the middle of the War Between the States, the Civil War, and the Union was struggling. The *New York Herald* quoted Lincoln's secretary of the interior as saying, "There was no disposition manifested by freedmen of the United States to leave the land of their nativity. Time will solve this question."

In the diary of Gideon Welles, secretary of the navy under Lincoln, there is a discussion at a Tuesday, February 2, 1864, cabinet meeting. President Lincoln and Seward, his secretary of state, seemed embarrassed by the scheme. The president appeared to decide to ignore the "Dominican Affair." (The Dominican Republic and Haiti are located on the same Hispaniola Island.)

This information and more, of course, is part of the basis of this book, *If You Please, President Lincoln*. I found the research fascinating. My characters demanded the right to tell the story from the viewpoint of the slaves, and I have filled in the gaps in the historical account with fiction.

I believe that any people's story is every people's story, and that from stories, we can all learn something to enrich our lives.

♦Bibliography

Basler, Roy P. *Collected Works of Abraham Lincoln: 1862–1863*. New Brunswick, N.J.: Rutgers University Press, 1953.

Beale, Howard K. *Diary of Gideon Welles* (Lincoln's Secretary of the Navy). New York, N.Y.: W. W. Norton, 1960.

Beale, Howard K. *Diary of Edward Bates* (Lincoln's Attorney General). Washington, D.C.: U.S. Government Printing Office, 1933.

Davis, Cyprian. *The History of Black Catholics*. New York, N.Y.: Crossroad Publishing Company, 1990.

Foner, Eric. *Reconstruction, American's Unfinished Revolution 1863–1877*. New York, N.Y.: Harper and Row, 1988.

Lorant, Stefan. *Lincoln: A Picture Story of His Life*. New York, N.Y.: Harper and Brothers, 1957.

Negro Colonization Schemes. New York Herald, Tuesday, March 22, 1864. Page 1, column 3.

Randall, J. G. *Lincoln the President, Springfield to Gettysburg*. Vol. 2. New York, N.Y.: Dodd, Mead and Company, 1945.

Weil, Thomas, et al. *Haiti: A Country Study—Foreign Area Studies*. Washington, D.C.: United States Government, Department of the Army, 1973.